MADGE HARRAH

My Brother, My Enemy

SIMON & SCHUSTER BOOKS FOR YOUNG READERS

SIMON & SCHUSTER BOOKS FOR YOUNG READERS
An imprint of Simon & Schuster Children's Publishing Division
1230 Avenue of the Americas, New York, New York 10020

SIMON & SCHUSTER BOOKS FOR YOUNG READERS is a trademark of
Simon & Schuster.

Book design by Anahid Hamparian
The text for this book is set in 12-point Kis
Printed and bound in the United States of America

First Edition
10 9 8 7 6 5 4 3 2 1
Library of Congress Cataloging-in-Publication Data
Harrah, Madge.
My brother, my enemy / Madge Harrah.
p.   cm.
Summary: Determined to avenge the massacre of his family, fourteen-year-old
Robert Bradford joins Nathaniel Bacon's rebel army in hopes of wiping out the
Susquehannock Indians of Virginia.
ISBN 0-689-80968-9
1. Bacon's Rebellion, 1676—Juvenile fiction. 2. Susquehanna Indians—Juvenile fiction.
3. Virginia—History—Colonial period,
ca. 1600–1775—Juvenile fiction. [1. Bacon's Rebellion, 1676—Fiction. 2. Susquehanna Indians—
Fiction. 3. Virginia—History—Colonial period, ca. 1600–1775—Fiction. 4. Indians of
North America—Virginia—Fiction.] I. Title.
PZ7.H2335My 1997
[Fic]—dc20 96-19963

For Larry

Preface

In 1676 in the colony of Virginia, there occurred an uprising now known as Bacon's Rebellion. Led by Nathaniel Bacon, a young firebrand who believed that Virginians should sever ties with England and rule themselves, the uprising lasted only a short time but produced several unusual incidents, including the infamous episode of the white aprons.

Opposing Bacon was Sir William Berkeley, governor of the colony and a loyal supporter of King Charles II. One of the officers in Berkeley's army was a man named John Washington. Before the rebellion ended, Berkeley and his men captured and hanged twenty-three of Bacon's followers, including Thomas Hansford and William Drummond. Hansford is now known as the first martyr to American liberty.

Despite the fact that Bacon's Rebellion failed, the seeds of independence were sown at that time. Exactly one hundred years later, in the same place for the same reasons, the descendants of the same people, including John Washington's great grandson George, started another uprising that became the American Revolution.

Treason doth never prosper: What's the reason?
For if it prosper, none dare call it treason.
Sir John Harington, 1561–1612

One

FOURTEEN YEARS OLD and sentenced to hang. In the morning. At dawn.

A sliver of moon smiles coldly through the bars. It makes me think of Aunt Charlotte, the way she smiles with her lips pressed together in a cold white curve just like that moon.

"Robert Bradford, you will hang before you reach your fifteenth birthday."

That's what she said to me back in June, soon after Nathaniel Bacon and his men found me upriver and brought me to Jamestown.

Now she has been proved right. She likes being right. Will she come tomorrow morning to watch when the hangman pulls the bench from beneath my feet? Will she smile when I struggle as the rope tightens?

Oh, God.

Earlier the guard gave me this pen, paper, a pot of ink.

"In case you want to write farewell notes to your friends and family," he said.

No knife, of course, to sharpen the quill. But what does it matter if this dull point smears the words? Aunt Charlotte will destroy anything I write. And neither Naokan nor Pomanah can read.

Did they escape? I wish I knew. It might help me face the morning if I knew they'd gotten away.

Now an owl is hooting out there in the night. Naokan once told me the Susquehannocks believe an owl is a messenger of death. My death? Their deaths? Please, God, let them reach the mountains ahead of the soldiers.

They'll never see this, but I'll write it anyway. Maybe that will help me understand the things that have happened. Not enough paper to write the whole story. When the paper runs out, I'll continue with memories. Six hours until dawn.

Naokan, my brother, my enemy. This is for you.

Four months ago. June 6, 1676. That's when it all started. I whistled happily that day as I headed home through the forest with my pistol stuck in my belt and the three squirrels I'd shot for supper in a sack slung over my shoulder. I was still a mile from home when I caught the first faint whiff of smoke.

Mother's already started the fire, I thought. She knows I'm on my way.

I pictured my mother, face flushed from the flames, stirring corn mush in the huge iron pot that hung from a chain in our fireplace. I saw my ten-year-old sister, Mary, placing pewter mugs and plates on the long table my father had made from split logs. I saw my baby brother, Charlie, playing near the fire with the toy horse I'd whittled for him from a pine bough the week before. I heard my father stamp across the porch, heard him call to my mother, "Anne, I'm home!"

My mouth watered, anticipating the good supper we'd soon have: buttery mush, fresh milk, fried squirrel.

The toe of my boot caught on a tree root and I pitched forward, landing on my knees in the moss that carpeted the ground. Just in front of me, half hidden by another root, lay an arrow. A Susquehannock arrow, tipped with flint and fletched with wild turkey feathers tied with red thread. My mother had given Naokan that thread during the winter. Now those red-banded arrows had become his special mark. Grinning, I scrambled to my feet and turned in a circle, searching the shadows.

"Naokan, I know you're here! Come on out!"

No answer. But the leaves of a nearby bush rustled as if stirred by wind in a spot where there was no wind. Still grinning, I charged toward the bush.

"Found you! You shouldn't have moved—"

A fox leapt out from behind the bush and dodged away through the trees. I looked around again, then glanced up, scanning the branches overhead. Instead of Naokan's face peering at me through the leaves, I saw dark tendrils of smoke curling through the treetops. Too much smoke, too black for a cook fire. I inhaled again and frowned as an acrid stench stung my nostrils. That was not the fresh, clean smell of the wood we burned in our fireplace.

"Father!"

Even as I cried out, I already knew. Dropping the bag of squirrels, I charged through the forest toward our cabin, the pistol gripped in my hand.

No, no, no . . .

The word pounded in my brain, keeping time with the pounding of my heart. I coughed, choking on the fumes that now greased the air.

No . . .

Branches whipped against my face. My cheeks stung. Lifting one arm to shield my eyes, I plunged ahead, crashing through the brush. By the time I broke free of the forest and entered our clearing near the river, my smoke-seared throat felt as raw as if it had been scraped with a knife. I stumbled to a halt, taking in the scene before me in one horrified, sweeping glance.

"No!"

The cabin, the barn, the tobacco shed. Gone. Nothing left but piles of flaming logs spewing black smoke into the sky.

Dashing forward, I knelt by my father's body. The hatchet that had split his skull lay beside him in a pool of blood. His blue eyes, fixed and glassy, stared sightlessly into mine. His stiffened fingers curled around the stock of his musket.

One musket against a Susquehannock war party. My hand tightened around my pistol. If only I had been there to help him. . . . But I couldn't think about that, not yet.

I swiveled about and stared toward the body of a Susquehannock warrior sprawled nearby. Okahanah, Naokan's uncle. The hole in his chest had obviously been made by a musket ball. My father had fired the musket, I decided, at the same moment that Okahanah had thrown the hatchet.

And just beyond Okahanah, lying on the ground, another arrow fletched with turkey feathers and tied with red thread.

Throwing back my head, I howled one last denial toward the sky. "No!"

I scrambled to my feet, looking frantically about the clearing. "Mother?"

She lay crumpled on the path to the tobacco shed, another of Naokan's arrows buried deep in her back. Near her sprawled the broken bodies of my brother and sister. My stomach convulsed, my knees buckled, pitching me forward into the dirt. Kneeling on all fours, I retched green bile.

My whole family, murdered by the Susquehannocks. By Naokan, who had sworn to be my brother.

I rose and turned from side to side, scanning the edges of the forest as I strained to catch the slap of moccasins, the snap of twigs, which might signal the war party's return. They would be back soon, I knew, to get Okahanah's body. The Susquehannocks never left their dead behind. Why had they done so now? Then I remembered the way I'd crashed through the underbrush in my flight toward home. They must have thought the whole Virginia army was on the march.

Kneeling, I pried the musket from my father's fingers.

"I'll be back," I told him. "This time I will have the soldiers with me."

I ran to the dock, which jutted like a long gray finger out into the sluggish expanse of the James River. Ignoring our sloop, which would be too hard for me to handle alone, I untied the dugout canoe that Naokan had helped me build. I placed the musket in the bottom of the canoe and turned for one last look at the carnage in the clearing. Rage boiled through my veins, a crimson flood.

"Naokan, hear me!" I shouted. "I am now your enemy!"

Using the skills that he had taught me, I paddled upriver toward the fort, cleaving the water with swift, silent strokes.

TWO

I'D GONE LESS than a mile when a sloop slid around the point ahead, its gray sails angling into the sky. Several men crowded the deck. Soldiers from the fort, I thought, coming to investigate the smoke.

"Here!" I shouted. "Over here!"

In response, one of the men on deck lifted his arm above his head and waved. I saw then that the men on the sloop were not soldiers, but planters, dressed in long flared coats and knee-high boots.

"Susquehannocks," I called, pointing back downriver. "They've killed my family."

"Susquehannocks!" exploded a man in a plumed hat. He took a pistol from his belt and fired it into the air. After a moment an answering shot echoed from beyond the point. A second sloop nosed into view.

"Hold fast, boy," called the man with the pistol. "We'll bring you aboard."

He barked orders to the other men, who scrambled about, adjusting sails to slow their speed. The second sloop slowed, too, and swung wide to give us room.

I maneuvered the canoe alongside the first sloop, which had a name painted on its bow: *Elizabeth*. A couple of the men dropped a rope ladder over the railing. One of them leaned down and extended a hand.

"Here, let me help you."

"Just take this."

I gave him the musket and scrambled up the ladder, canoe rope in hand. When I reached the deck, the other man grabbed the rope and trailed the canoe toward the stern. To my surprise, my knees buckled. I sank down on a pile of canvas, breathing hard. Several men gathered around, but were pushed aside by a slim, brown-haired man.

"Robert?"

Surprised to hear my name, I peered toward a lean face that seemed familiar. For a moment I couldn't pull forth the name. Then it came to me—Thomas Hansford, a planter who had visited my father two months before.

"What happened?" he asked.

I swallowed hard before I could speak the words. "Father's dead. Murdered by Susquehannocks. Mother, too. Mary and Charlie. I was coming to get the soldiers to help me—" I took a deep breath, trying to steady my voice. "To help me bury them."

"Faugh! The soldiers!" The man with the pistol spat out the words like a curse. His deep-set eyes, so dark a blue they looked almost black, burned into mine. "You're certain the Indians were Susquehannocks?"

"Yes."

"Why were you spared?"

"I wasn't there when . . . I'd been out hunting. I came home and found—" Again I had to pause before I could go on. "Found my family dead. Along with the body of a Susquehannock warrior. My father had shot him."

I dropped my head to hide the tears, which threatened to overflow. Hansford placed a hand on my shoulder. "This is a hard thing, Robert."

I nodded, still unable to speak.

"More than fifty Virginians murdered by the Indians in the past three months," cried the man with the pistol. "How many more, Hansford? How many must die before that old fool in Jamestown takes action?"

Caught by the rage that shook the man's voice, I looked up to find his dark eyes burning into mine.

"Doegs," he said. "Those are the Indians that killed my overseer. They killed the Robert Hen family, too. Seventeen other families, murdered by Doegs and Occaneechis. Now your family, murdered by the Susquehannocks. If all the tribes unite against us—"

Acid burned my throat as I pictured all tribes banding together to destroy us. They could do it, too, with their knowledge of the wilderness.

"Berkeley must let us fight. If he doesn't, we'll fight anyway." The man slammed his fist against the railing.

"I'm with you, Bacon!" shouted one of the men.

"So am I," shouted another.

"No, Nathaniel, wait." Hansford stepped forward, his face knotted like a fist. "We must get the commission first."

Nathaniel Bacon.

Now I remembered. I'd overheard Hansford and my father talking about a man with that name, something about Bacon's trying to get permission from Governor Berkeley in Jamestown to raise his own army to protect the plantations against attack.

I rose to my feet. My own fists curled, my heart pounded. "Let's go after them now."

All I wanted was one shot. One shot straight into Naokan's heart.

Bacon eyed the sky where the smoke drifted like a gauzy curtain, filming the sun.

"How long since the attack?" he asked.

"I don't know. At least an hour."

"They never leave their dead behind. Why—?"

"When I smelled the smoke I headed for home at a dead run. I made so much noise—"

"They thought the soldiers were coming." He glanced toward Hansford and snorted, a bitter laugh that held no humor. "Berkeley's men stamp through the forest like a herd of horses. No wonder they never catch the Indians."

"But we could catch them now," I said, stepping forward. "I know where the Susquehannock village is."

In my mind I watched Naokan jerk and fall as a musket ball shattered his chest.

"How far?"

"Four hours' march—"

Hansford grabbed Bacon's arm. "Nathaniel, we have to get to Jamestown. We're a day late already."

"We could be there by dark," I said. "We could surprise them."

Bacon looked back and forth between Hansford and me, his face tight.

"The Assembly has already gathered, you know that," Hansford said. "If we don't show up to counter Berkeley's accusations, he could charge us with treason. Nathaniel, he could hang us all."

The two men stood without moving, their eyes locked.

"Your commission, Nathaniel," Hansford said at last. "We'll get the commission and then—"

After a moment, Bacon nodded, his face grim.

"Then we'll come back and kill every Susquehannock in Virginia."

Kill every Susquehannock.

Pomanah's face rose before me. Pomanah, Naokan's sister. Trilling laughter, sparkling eyes, a body as strong and lithe as a deer. I'd watched her splint a robin's broken leg, hide a fawn from hunters. She would have taken no part in the murder of my family. Until today, I would have sworn that Naokan would have done no such thing, either.

But those arrows tied with red thread had been his. Or . . . the thought chilled my blood . . . those arrows had been mine. Just the month before I'd sat with him in his village and helped him twine red thread around the shafts of a new set of arrows while Pomanah stirred a pot of soup over the fire. Okahanah, the war chief, had squatted nearby, glaring at me through slitted eyes.

"White soldiers killed our five chiefs. All white men are bad. All white men must die," he had growled at last.

Then he had risen and stalked off while Naokan, Pomanah, and I had stared uneasily at each other.

Now I stared at Nathaniel Bacon. The same anger, the same violence, flamed in him that I'd seen in Okahanah, yet power radiated from him, too, a strength that drew me as a magnet draws iron.

"You're right, we must face Berkeley," he said to Hansford. Turning to me, he added, "But first we will bury your family."

He shouted orders to the men on both sloops. They scrambled about, pulling on ropes and adjusting the sails until the sloops glided forward like geese. I paced the deck and scanned the shore for any sign of movement among the trees. The muscles tightened in my chest, tensing against the possible *thwack* of an arrow.

When we reached our landing area, the men dropped anchor and went ashore in rowboats while I followed in the canoe. Tattered wisps of smoke still drifted overhead. I tied the canoe to the wharf and scrambled up, charging after the men as they loped forward, muskets and shovels in their hands. Nausea gripped me again when I entered the clearing and once more viewed my family's bodies.

"Savages," Bacon growled.

He dropped his shovel and strode forward to kneel beside my father. I'd suspected that Okahanah's body would be gone by the time we got there, and it was, along with the hatchet and Naokan's arrows.

Hansford appeared beside me.

"Where do you want them buried?"

I pointed toward a large oak tree that rose at the edge of the forest.

"There. My father loved that oak. Bury them there."

Two hours later I stood, dry-eyed, beside the graves. The men waited nearby, their hats doffed, their heads bowed.

"Lord, here lie four good people," I said. "Please welcome them into your kingdom."

"Amen," chorused the men.

"Do you have any other family?" Bacon asked.

"Just one aunt, my mother's sister. Charlotte Bromworth. She lives in Jamestown."

And she hates me, I added silently, remembering that awful scene five years before when she had ordered my father and me out of her house.

But I didn't voice my doubts out loud. After all, she was the only relative I had left. It seemed fitting that I should be the one to tell her what had happened.

"Then you will sail to Jamestown with us," Bacon said.

We did not try to sail down the river in the dark but remained tied up near shore until daybreak. I'm not sure any of those men slept that night. I did sleep some, a fitful sleep, waking from time to time to listen to the talk around me. I learned that Bacon and his men had tried to get permission during the winter from Governor Berkeley to raise their own army to fight the Indians and had been denied. I learned that they had raised an army anyway and had already fought one battle with the Doegs. I learned that many victims, including women and children, had been tortured to death by the Indians in terrible ways.

At least my family had died quickly and had not been tortured.

In the morning the winds proved fair and we made good time. As we sailed into Jamestown harbor at noon, Bacon stood at the helm and announced in ringing tones, "Now, men, we will bring that old fool Berkeley to his knees!"

Then I watched the look of triumph on his face change to anger and dismay.

"Villainy!" he cried.

I turned to see a warship bearing down upon us. The deck bloomed with soldiers, the gun ports bristled with cannon.

"Hold or we'll blow you out of the water!" shouted an officer from the other ship. "You are all under arrest!"

Three

"**PUT ABOUT!**" Bacon shouted. "Make a run for it!"

Everyone on both sloops scrambled to adjust the sails as several shots from the warship's cannons struck the water around us, sending up geysers of spray.

"When we shoot again we'll sink you," shouted the officer from the ship. "Put ashore at once."

"Perdition!" Bacon exploded. "All right, men, put ashore."

When we landed we were met by a battalion of armed soldiers led by a cold-eyed officer.

"Major Hone," Bacon said, surveying the officer with obvious contempt.

"Mr. Bacon. You and your men will accompany us to the gaol."

"Let the boy go," Bacon said. "He's not a part of this."

"He's with you now. The governor says to put your men in the gaol and bring you and Hansford before the Assembly."

Without further words he marched us all through the streets of Jamestown to the gaol. When the soldiers began shoving us into the small brick-lined cells, Hone said, gesturing toward Bacon and Hansford, "Shackle those two."

"Bring the boy along," Bacon said. "I'll explain to Berkeley that he's not with my army."

Hone shrugged as if it were of no interest to him. "Until then, we'll have to shackle him, too."

Soldiers stepped forward to lock heavy iron cuffs connected by chains around our wrists and ankles. The weight dragged at my arms, pulling my head and shoulders forward.

"Come along," said Hone as he prodded us with his sword. "The Assembly is waiting."

We stumbled out into the sunlight, escorted by Hone and four soldiers with guns held ready. Angry cries rose behind us from the men in the gaol.

"Berkeley should be in this gaol, not us."

"We're loyal citizens—"

Shuffling down the dusty road, I felt as if I were trapped in a nightmare, wanting to run but unable to lift my feet.

I glanced toward two women who stood together on the front stoop of a house, their eyes fixed upon us as they whispered behind their hands.

Further down the road a man in a flared coat and plumed hat, his face agleam with curiosity, addressed a companion while gesturing toward us with a curved clay pipe.

"The surly one in the middle, that's Bacon," he said.

"Who's the boy?"

"Another rebel. Looks to be a hard one."

A rebel.

The shackles bowed my back, as if I had indeed done something wrong and were now dragged down by shame. I peered ahead, trying to locate the State House.

In my mind I saw my father stand before me, as he had many years ago, handsome in his blue coat and beaver hat, his face glowing with pride.

"That is the State House," he had said while pointing toward a large brick structure. "When you grow up you may get elected to serve there. Just think, the son of a former indentured servant—a councilman!"

I tightened my lips, imagining his grief in Heaven as he now looked down to watch me stumbling toward the State House in chains.

"Bacon, Bacon!" Snorting through their noses, three small boys dashed into the street. "Oink! Oink! Bacon is a pig!"

They picked up rocks and flung them hard, striking me in the knee and hitting Bacon on the arm. One of the boys looked like Charlie. I swallowed against the grief that clogged my throat.

"Halt!" shouted Major Hone.

The soldiers snapped to attention, their guns angled across their chests.

The State House loomed before us, unrelenting in its symmetry.

"Stand guard outside," Hone said, addressing two of the soldiers. "You," he said to the other two, "follow us inside."

Major Hone led the way up the steps and pushed open the large front doors. We struggled after him, encumbered by the chains that bound our ankles. We entered a large hallway, which was flanked on either side by tall double doors. A staircase rose before us from the center of the hallway toward the upper story.

"Courage, Robert," Bacon murmured as I turned my head toward the doors to our right from which issued the muffled buzzing of voices, sounding like cicadas in August. Major Hone knocked upon those doors and the buzzing ceased.

The man who opened the doors looked us over, then turned and announced in a loud voice, "My Lord Governor Berkeley, Major Hone is here with the rebel leaders."

"Bring them in."

My heart raced, my pulse pounded in my ears. When I entered the room I saw nothing but a blur of white faces, a merging of coats and vests in a wave of peacock colors. Then my vision cleared. On the platform at the front of the room stood an older man, his florid face mirroring the red of the sash that slashed diagonally across his green vest. I absorbed the rest of his costume in one quick glance: long curly wig spilling down around his shoulders, blue velvet coat and breeches, shoes with silver buckles.

If that was Governor Berkeley, he was nothing but a popinjay, I thought with disdain.

Then he spoke, his voice hard, and I shivered at the power I heard in those cold tones.

"Nathaniel Bacon and Thomas Hansford. You've sailed straight into our net."

Bacon took a step forward, his chin held high. "I am an elected member of this council. I've come to take my rightful place in this Assembly."

Berkeley's face flushed a deeper red. "Your rightful place is at the end of a rope."

Alarm scurried down my spine like a swarm of ants. Bacon stood unwavering, his eyes fixed upon Berkeley. An elderly man rose from one of the nearby seats, his craggy face tight with anger.

"If it weren't for Bacon's action against the Indians, my plantation would be ashes by now," he said.

"Sit down, Mr. Presley," Berkeley commanded.

The old man huffed through his nose like a horse and remained standing, his chin lifted in obvious defiance. Bacon made his way down the aisle, chains clanking with every step. He planted himself before Berkeley, shoulders back, head high.

"My men and I defended our homes on the strength of your promised commission," he said. "I demand to have that commission now."

"I gave you no commission," Berkeley replied.

"You told me two months ago that you would," Bacon stated firmly. "I expected you, as a gentleman, to keep your word."

I could tell that the shot hit home. My father had once told me that Governor Berkeley prided himself above all else on being a gentleman.

"You, as a gentleman, should have waited until you received your official commission," Berkeley countered. "Instead, you gathered an army and marched on your own, knowing full well your actions were illegal. Virginia already has an army—"

"A useless army led by fools," snorted Presley. He pointed toward a large man wearing the red, blue, and gold uniform of an army officer. "There's your culprit. We wouldn't be in this trouble now if John Washington over there hadn't shot those five Susquehannock chiefs under a flag of truce. No wonder the Susquehannocks have gone on the warpath."

The large man sprang to his feet, his eyes blazing. "It was the militia from Maryland that killed those five chiefs!"

Presley surveyed him with a cynical expression. "That's your story."

"Sit down, Mr. Presley. You, too, Colonel Washington," Berkeley commanded firmly.

Presley thudded back into his seat, his jaw clenched, his brows tight. Washington lowered himself into his chair with somewhat more dignity, but his face remained stormy.

"As I was saying, we have the army, we have the forts—" Berkeley began.

"Robert, come forward," Bacon interrupted, fastening me with his dark, hypnotic eyes.

I stumbled down the aisle to join him, my heart hammering against my ribs.

"This is Robert Bradford," Bacon announced. "Yesterday his entire family was massacred by the Susquehannocks and his home was burned. Tell them, Robert, how Berkeley's soldiers helped you."

His voice grated with sarcasm.

"Our la—land . . ." I stopped, swallowed, and began again. "Our land lies two miles downriver from one of the forts. The Susquehannocks slipped right by the fort. They killed my family. They burned all our buildings. They slaughtered our livestock. Yet the soldiers from the fort never came."

"We saw the smoke," Bacon said. "My men and I, as we came downriver, *we* saw the smoke. Where, Governor Berkeley, were the soldiers from the fort?"

Ignoring Bacon's question, Berkeley stared down at me. To my surprise I saw the hard look in his eyes give way to compassion.

"You lost your entire family?" he asked.

"Yes, Sir. My mother and father. My younger sister and brother."

"You are not one of Bacon's men?"

"He is not," Bacon declared before I could answer. "Because he had nowhere else to go, we brought him with us to Jamestown."

"Release this boy," Berkeley said, glancing toward Major Hone.

Hone gestured toward one of the soldiers, who stepped forward and unlocked the shackles, one by one. As they fell away, I rubbed the ache in my wrists.

"Release Bacon, too," Presley demanded, once more rising to his feet.

"That I cannot do, not yet." Berkeley surveyed Bacon through narrowed eyes. "If you kneel before this Assembly, confess yourself a rebel, acknowledge me as the leader of Virginia and ask forgiveness, I will then reconsider granting you a commission."

Bacon drew back, his face dark. "Kneel before you? No."

An older man rose and approached the platform. "If it please Your Honor, may I speak with my cousin alone?"

"Mr. Bacon," Berkeley said, acknowledging the older man. Turning back to the younger Bacon, Berkeley said, "Your cousin wishes to counsel with you. Do I have your word as a gentleman that you will not attempt to flee?"

"Yes," Bacon replied, "for I know that a gentleman's word is worth more than gold. A gentleman's word is his honor. Just as you gave me your gentleman's word two months ago concerning my commission."

"Hear, hear!" shouted Presley.

Bacon shuffled from the room, followed by his elderly cousin. I looked around the room at the other assemblymen. One delegate, his face as sharp as that of a fox, leaned back casually in his chair. A slight smile lifted one corner of his mouth. All the other delegates sat forward, faces strained, bodies perched on the edges of their seats. The air in the room seemed to crackle with energy, just as air tingles before a thunderstorm, lifting the hair on one's arms.

"Go," Hansford told me.

I followed Bacon and his cousin into the front hallway. They were already engaged in heated conversation by the time I arrived.

"—will not kneel," Bacon said.

The older man lifted his chin, his craggy face tight with tension. "Which means more to you, Nathaniel, your pride or your life?"

I slid along one wall, thinking to slip out through the front doors, but when I opened those doors, I saw that Berkeley's soldiers were still standing guard outside. What if they shot me, thinking I was trying to escape? Hastily I closed the doors again.

"Listen to me." His cousin stepped forward and grasped Bacon's arm. "Berkeley has declared all of you rebels, which takes away your right to hold land. Unless you compromise, you and your men and their families will end up homeless. And you as their leader—Berkeley will hang you if you don't back down. Think of your own children. Think of your wife."

For the first time I saw Bacon waver. "When we left England I promised Elizabeth a fine life here in the New World."

"You've put Berkeley in a bad position. He *is* the governor here, and he represents King Charles. You've challenged his authority and he has to take action. This is a way out for you both. If you kneel and recite a few words, you get your army, which is what you wanted in the first place."

Bacon pulled from his cousin's grasp and paced away. That brought him face-to-face to me. He paused, looking surprised, as if he'd forgotten I was there.

"Robert, what do you think I should do?"

Images flashed through my mind: my father's sightless eyes, my mother's broken body. Hatred for Naokan surged through me like poison. "I don't care how you do it, just get your army and go after the Susquehannocks."

The older man stepped forward and again grasped Bacon's arm. "To kneel takes courage. Are you that brave?"

"You want me to compromise."

"You're as close to a son as I'll ever have. I want you to live."

The two men stood for a long moment with their eyes locked. Finally Bacon's shoulders sagged.

"All right," he said.

The two of them reentered the assembly room and I followed, pausing beside Hansford. He glanced at me, his question obvious: *Is he going to do it?*

I nodded.

"So, Mr. Bacon, what is your decision?" asked Berkeley.

Looking neither to the right nor left, Bacon made his way to the front of the room and sank to his knees before the platform. "I hereby confess that I have been guilty of unlawful and rebellious action. For this I entreat the pardon of God and of this Assembly."

Triumph flared across Berkeley's face. "There is joy in Heaven when a sinner repents. God forgive you. I forgive you."

"And all who were with me," Bacon said firmly.

"And all who were with you," Berkeley echoed. "Major Hone, release Bacon and his men."

Bacon rose and turned, his face a mask carved from stone.

"This session is adjourned," Berkeley announced. "We will meet here again this afternoon."

I listened to the scornful comments that surged through the room.

"—would never have guessed Bacon was a coward."

"Berkeley's clever . . ."

On Hone's command, the soldier who had released me now stepped forward and removed Bacon's shackles. As soon as he'd been set free, Bacon marched down the aisle, eyes focused straight ahead as if no one else in the room existed. He passed Hansford and me with no comment, just one quick glance. The assemblymen, still buzzing among themselves, rose but made no effort to push into the aisles until Hone had removed Hansford's cuffs.

"Come," Hansford said, grabbing my arm and pulling me with him from the room.

We caught up with Bacon on the front steps of the State House where he stood with his shoulders slumped and his fists clenched.

"It's all right, Nathaniel," Hansford said. "I understand why you did it."

Bacon glanced our way, his eyes bleak. "Compromise."

Hansford grimaced. "I know all about compromise. Every one of us has had to compromise at one time or another."

Bacon shook his head. "You can't compromise your honor and remain the same man."

"But you do have your army," I reminded him. "Now you can destroy the Susquehannocks."

Bacon straightened his shoulders. "Robert, you're right. Come, Hansford, we'll escort this boy to his aunt's home and then go see that our men are released."

Aunt Charlotte.

The loss of my family closed around me, a choking fog. Aunt Charlotte's cruel words to my father so long ago once more rang in my ears: "I despise you, John Bradford, for taking away my sister. You're killing her out there in that wilderness, you know that. Hard work. No servants. Too many children." She shot an angry glance in my direction, including me in the blame. "Anne is always welcome here, but you are not. Do not visit me again."

For a brief moment I considered staying away from Aunt Charlotte. Almost immediately I put the thought from my mind. As my mother's only sister she had a right to hear of the murders from me, rather than from some town gossip.

"She lives in the last brick house on the east edge of town," I said.

I led the way, my wrists now shackled with dread.

Four

WHEN AUNT CHARLOTTE opened the door and saw me standing on the stoop, the lines on either side of her pinched mouth deepened as if she had just been slashed by a knife.

"You!"

How she could compress so much dislike into one word amazed me.

"Mother is dead," I told her flatly. "Father, too. Mary and Charlie."

Her pale face turned as gray as stale bread dough. She reached out one hand and grasped the doorjamb for support.

"They were killed by Susquehannocks. Yesterday," I went on, still speaking without emotion.

She took a deep shuddering breath. "I knew it," she said. "I knew something like this would happen. How—how did you—?"

"I'd been out hunting. I came home and found them. But they—I was too late."

"He killed her," she said flatly.

"Who—?"

"John Bradford killed my sister."

"No, I told you, it was the Susque—"

"*He* killed her," she interrupted. "He is the one who led her into danger. Anne, my sweet Anne . . ."

Her voice faltered and she closed her eyes, still clinging to the doorjamb. After a moment she released her hold upon the door and straightened her shoulders in an obvious struggle to bring herself under control. She opened her eyes and glanced toward Bacon and Hansford, who waited nearby in the road.

"I know who you are," she told them in a stiff voice. "I should have expected to find this boy in such company."

"They came by yesterday and helped me dig the graves—" My voice broke at last. I swallowed hard and pressed my lips together, determined not to weaken in front of her.

"Where are they buried?"

"Under an oak tree on our land."

A quiver shook her body, belying her lifted chin and tight face.

"Was a clergyman present to perform the service?" she asked.

"No."

She surveyed me for a long moment in silence. Then she stood aside, unblocking the door.

"I suppose you'd better come in."

I turned toward Bacon and Hansford. "Thank you."

Hansford's brows pulled together in obvious concern. "Will you be all right?"

"Yes."

I had no idea if that were true, but I felt they had done enough for me. Turning, I edged past Aunt Charlotte. She closed the door and led the way into the sitting room. I thought she was going to sit down in one of the gilt chairs, but she remained standing, her head thrown back, her jaws clenched.

I knew she was only five years older than my mother, which would make her thirty-seven, but the bitter lines that edged her mouth made her look much older. Everything about her shouted of wealth: the jewels in her elaborate wig, the gleaming lace and satin of her gown, the blue silk shoes that peeked from beneath her skirts. My mother had owned no wig but had let her soft brown hair flow about her shoulders. The arrow that killed her had pierced a dress of simple homespun.

I glanced toward a portrait in oils that hung on one wall, a large portrait in an ornate gilt frame. Lord Bromworth, my grandfather, a Cavalier who had immigrated to Virginia during England's civil war. He had died of apoplexy three months before I was born.

"Anne's marriage killed our father," Aunt Charlotte said, following my gaze. "Now it has killed her, too."

"My mother—," I began.

"I rue the day John Bradford came into our lives." Her voice stung with bitterness.

"My mother and father loved each other," I finished, determined to defend them.

One corner of Aunt Charlotte's thin mouth curled in a sneer. "Your father —our indentured servant. Deported from England for theft."

"He was innocent."

"So he always claimed." Again her eyes swept over me without warmth. "You look just like him. Same brown hair, same stubborn jaw. When he took Anne away—" She paused before going on. "I warned her. And now . . . "

Her face suddenly crumpled like a collapsing rock wall. Tears welled in her eyes and spilled over, tracking rivulets through the white powder that dusted her face. She groped for a chair and sank down upon the embroidered cushion. Lowering her face into her hands, she wept, calling my mother's name. The heartbreak in her voice stabbed through me. I stepped forward and touched her shoulder, trying to offer her the comfort she had denied me. She flinched as if I had brushed her with a hot coal. Rising, she moved toward the doorway.

"Come," she said, "I will take you to the kitchen. Joanna will feed you while I . . . we shall see."

She led me from the main house to a second, smaller house out back. The smell of fresh-baked bread wafted through the open doorway of that house. As we entered, the heat from the roaring fireplace struck my skin like a blast from the gates of Hell. A scrawny woman, silhouetted against the glare of the flames, shoved a long-handled wooden paddle into the fireplace oven and withdrew a steaming loaf, which she placed on the wooden table that filled the center of the room.

"Joanna, this is my nephew, Robert Bradford," Aunt Charlotte said. "Give him some food. I'll be back soon."

She stalked away, back stiff, head high. Joanna glanced toward me, her pockmarked face flushed red from the heat.

"Help yourself. Stew is in the pot." Her drawling voice suggested she had been born in an English slum. She pointed toward an iron pot suspended from a rod between two tall iron firedogs near the fireplace.

It had been many hours since Bacon and his men had shared their cheese and bread with me on board the sloop. I took an earthenware bowl from a nearby shelf and stepped forward to ladle out the stew. Steam, rising from the pot, filled my nostrils with the rich aroma of mutton and cabbage. Suddenly ravenous, I sat down at the table, picked up a spoon that lay there, and began to eat.

"You her sister's child?" Joanna asked.

"Yes," I mumbled around a mouthful of stew.

She turned and fixed me with a questioning look. "I was in the market when the soldiers arrested Bacon's men. I saw you with them."

"Yes."

She stood, obviously waiting for more.

"Berkeley has pardoned Bacon," I told her. "We've been released."

"Why are you here?"

"Susquehannocks killed my family yesterday. I thought Aunt Charlotte should know."

"Her sister is dead, then." There was no pity in her voice.

Although I had met Amos, Aunt Charlotte's slave who lived in a cabin near the stables, this woman I had never seen before.

"Joanna, are you—?"

"Yes, I'm indentured to her," she interrupted, anticipating my question. "I have three years to go before my bondage ends."

"Are you a redemptioner?"

"No." She held up her right hand to show me the T for thief that had been branded into her palm. I knew that redemptioners, who sold themselves into servitude for passage to the New World, bore no such brands.

"My father's palm was branded with the same mark," I said.

Something shifted in her eyes, a reassessment, as if that information made us allies.

"Where are you from?" I continued.

"London. My son . . . he was two years old. He was sick and we hadn't eaten for three days. I thought a little broth . . . I stole a hen."

She paused, her eyes unfocused, her mouth open. I could tell she was lost in memory.

"What happened?" I asked.

"They caught me. They could have hanged me, you know." I nodded.

"The judge was merciful." She laughed, a cynical snort without humor. "He sentenced me to seven years in the colonies."

"And your son?"

"He died the day after I'd been arrested."

She stated the words without emotion, but her eyes were open wounds. Grief for my own family throbbed inside me like a boil.

"What is it like, serving my aunt?"

She shrugged. "It could be worse. Josiah Wheeler, the blacksmith here, killed his indentured apprentice last week. An accident, he said, but some of us know better."

She turned away and lifted another loaf from the oven.

Appetite gone, I pushed the bowl to one side. When a shadow fell across the table, I rose to see my aunt standing in the doorway, a blue silk cloak about her shoulders and a tall silk bonnet trimmed in black lace perched atop her wig.

"I have an errand in town," she said to me. "You will wait here until I return."

As she turned and hurried away the cloak swished behind her like a sweep of rain.

Joanna laughed, one brief bark without humor. "She doesn't like you."

"You're right. Thank you for the stew."

I stepped out into the yard, seeking a breeze to relieve the suffocating heat of the kitchen. Amos, his dark skin glistening with sweat in the afternoon sunshine, his large hands gripping the handle of a hoe, chopped at weeds in the kitchen garden.

My father had hated all forms of servitude, but he had hated slavery most of all.

I walked over to the garden.

"Hello, Amos."

He paused and peered at me for a moment before recognition dawned. "Master Robert, it is you."

He spoke with a rhythmical accent that carried the sound of drums.

"Yes. How are you, Amos?"

He did not answer. Instead, his black eyes, deepset in a chiseled face, took my measure. "You have grown. I did not know you."

"It's been five years."

"Mistress Anne? . . . ." He paused, letting the question trail away when I shook my head.

"Amos, she's dead. Killed yesterday by the Indians. Father and Mary and Charlie, too."

He lowered his head and stood in silence for a long moment. There was a dignity about him, a brooding sense of power. He had once told me he'd been king of his tribe back in Africa before the slavers captured him. The livid scars that slashed his face and arms gave evidence of the battle he'd put up that day.

He lifted his head once more, his expression fierce. "Your father fought them."

I nodded. "He killed their war chief."

"That is good."

He faced me as an equal, one man to another, honoring my father's courage. I felt more comfort in his respect than I had felt at any other moment during the preceding twenty-four hours.

I picked up a second hoe that was lying on the ground and entered the garden. Amos accepted my presence without question. Together we set to work on the weeds, chopping in silence.

The sun was descending toward the horizon when my aunt returned. She approached the garden, calling sharply. "Robert!"

I put down the hoe and advanced to meet her.

"I have found a position for you here in town with a man who will teach you a trade," she said.

"A trade?"

"Yes. You cannot run a plantation by yourself, not with marauding Indians, and you certainly can't stay here. Therefore, I've spoken with a worthy tradesman here in town who has agreed to take you on as apprentice, a man who is currently without a helper."

My skin prickled with forewarning. "Who is this tradesman?"

"His name," said my aunt, "is Josiah Wheeler."

Five

ALL THE GRIEF and frustration of the past two days welled up in one defiant burst: "No!"

Aunt Charlotte's eyes narrowed. "I'm trying to help you, Robert. To work with Josiah Wheeler is a fine opportunity."

I remembered my father's words from long ago: *Better to die in freedom than to live in bondage.*

I glanced toward Amos, once a king, now a slave.

"Thank you, Aunt Charlotte, but I'm going home."

"Back to the plantation by yourself?"

"My hands are strong." I lifted them to show her. "Our summer tobacco is already planted. I'll harvest it alone."

Foolish words. Most plantations required at least a dozen slaves and indentured servants to tend to all the work. My father and I, laboring together with no extra help, had been hard pressed to keep up with the plowing, the planting, the harvesting, the hunting, the fishing, the construction of new buildings.

"We work hard, but we're free," my father had reminded me after we'd finished adding a new porch to our cabin. "Our labor belongs to us, not someone else. Therein lies the difference."

Now our cabin lay in ruins and my family moldered beneath the earth. I looked at Aunt Charlotte's hands, smooth and white. I thought of my mother's hands, calloused by toil but always tender in her loving care of us all. Rage at her death exploded inside me.

"But before going home I shall join Bacon's army and kill every Susquehannock I can find!"

Aunt Charlotte's face tightened into harsh lines. "Bacon is

a scofflaw. Join with him, Robert Bradford, and you will hang before you reach your fifteenth birthday."

"Perhaps the Indians will kill me first."

"Perhaps they will."

We faced each other across a chasm that held no bridge.

I turned back toward Amos and lifted one hand in farewell. "Good-bye."

He did not reply but stood, tall and straight, a dark silhouette against the sky. I left them both and hurried toward the river, squinting against the glare of late afternoon sunlight that glanced off the waves and pierced my eyes like swords. What if I were too late? What if Bacon had already sailed?

My heart lifted when I spotted his sloop, straining at its anchor rope as it rocked on the tide near one of the wharves.

"Where's Bacon?" I called to a man on deck. "Are you sailing soon?"

"No." The man hawked and spat over the side of the boat into the water. "That's one for Berkeley's eye. The old fool is dragging his feet on writing the commission."

"But he promised—"

"Aye, he did. He promised a lot of things."

"Where is Bacon, then?"

"That way." He pointed toward the town. "Inn and tavern run by a man named Richard Lawrence. Look there."

I left the river and hurried in the direction the man had indicated. Six of Berkeley's soldiers, muskets tilted against their shoulders, swords hanging from their baldrics, came toward me down the middle of the street. I stepped aside as they tramped past.

"Looks to me as if they're expecting trouble," said a gruff voice behind me. I turned to see old Mr. Presley leaning against a tree, his arms folded across his chest.

"Good evening, Sir."

He straightened and peered more closely at my face. "I

remember you. You're that boy who was with Bacon today."

"Yes, Sir. I'm looking for Richard Lawrence's inn. Do you know where it is?"

"That's where I'm staying. Come along."

He pushed off down the street, threading his way through clusters of men. Here and there I caught snatches of conversation.

"— can't wait any longer. We must defend ourselves."

"The Indians—"

"— four more murders."

"Why doesn't Berkeley act?"

"— friends with the Indians."

"— getting rich off the beaver trade. He's besotted over that young wife of his. Wants to keep her in jewels."

"Lady Berkeley is a beautiful woman."

"Philip Ludwell certainly thinks so."

As guffaws echoed down the street, Mr. Presley chuckled, too.

"So, Philip Ludwell lusts after Berkeley's wife. Well, I'll tell you this, if I were twenty years younger and Lady Berkeley were ten years older, I'd go after her myself." He paused before a two-story brick house. "Here we are."

The door at the top of the steps had been propped open with a stool. We mounted the steps and entered a large smoky room with a beamed ceiling. I stepped into the shadows near the door while I took in the scene.

Bacon and Hansford sat at a table near the fireplace. They scowled toward another table, which was occupied by Colonel Washington and a handsome, well-dressed man I didn't know, although I had seen him earlier that day in the State House. Even as we entered, Colonel Washington lifted a glass in a salute toward Bacon and Hansford while addressing his companion.

"We drink, Mr. Ludwell, in air made pure by the prayers of penitent sinners."

"I will not take this," Bacon growled. Fists clenched, he started to rise.

Hansford reached out and grabbed his arm. Lifting his own glass toward the other table, he said, "My prayers, Colonel Washington, are for you and your friend and those five Susquehannock chiefs who now approach Heaven waving a white flag."

Washington slammed his glass down on the table. "I keep telling you, it was the militia from Maryland that killed those five chiefs!"

Mr. Presley strode forward, cackling with obvious glee. "Stick with that story and maybe someday someone will believe you."

Plunking himself down on a bench near Bacon and Hansford, Presley lifted one hand and motioned to an aproned man who stood near a counter laden with bottles. "Whiskey, Mr. Lawrence."

The man picked up a glass and bottle and hurried forward, a sly smile on his face. "Here you are, Mr. Presley."

Where had I seen that smile before? Then I remembered the man in the State House who had leaned back and smiled after Bacon had made his confession.

"Come, boy," Presley called, motioning for me to join him.

I saw Bacon's eyebrows shoot up with surprise when I left the shadows to sit beside Presley on the bench. Before Bacon could say anything, however, Presley took a deep drink of the whiskey and then choked, a series of gasps that made him sound as if he were about to expire.

"Almost as good as what I make back home," he wheezed at last.

Hansford leaned forward and surveyed Presley with obvious interest. "Where are you from, Mr. Presley?"

"Northampton. I got elected to this Assembly because I'm old and mean and speak my mind." He set down his glass and began counting off grievances on his gnarled fingers. "Unfair taxes . . . unfair trade laws . . . the Indian attacks." Brows bristling, he glared at Ludwell and Washington. "Berkeley's a fool if he thinks those Indian attacks are over. I'm here to see some changes made in the way this colony is run."

Ludwell reared back, his chest swelling like a toad's. "This is an English colony, subject to the king. Are you loyal to the king?"

"That depends. Is the king loyal to me?"

Ludwell's face hardened. "That sounds seditious. Be careful, Mr. Presley."

"You're the one who should be careful, courting Berkeley's wife. What kind of loyalty lies in that?"

With an oath, Ludwell jumped up and reached for his sword. As his thigh bumped the table, a bottle toppled over splashing his satin coat and lace cuffs with wine.

Washington also leapt to his feet and circled the table to pinion Ludwell's arms. "Let it go, Philip. He's just an old man."

By then both Bacon and Hansford had also risen to their feet, and so had I. Presley, still seated on the bench, sipped his whiskey while eyeing Ludwell calmly as if nothing were happening.

"Gentlemen, gentlemen! It's too fine an evening to quarrel." Lawrence hurried forward with a fresh bottle of wine. His lips drew back in a smile, but his eyes held a calculating gleam.

"Come, Philip," Washington said, releasing Ludwell's arms. "We'll find better company elsewhere."

"Richer, maybe," Presley rejoined, "but no better."

For a moment Ludwell continued to glare at Presley. Then he stalked toward the door, chin high, eyes focused straight ahead. Washington tossed a couple of coins onto the table. When the coins rolled off onto the floor, he did not stoop to pick them up but followed Ludwell from the tavern.

Presley laughed and slapped his thigh. "The fancy Mr.

Ludwell will have to change his clothes before visiting the governor's lady this evening."

Lawrence grinned. "I believe Berkeley arrested the wrong rebel, Mr. Presley."

Ignoring them both, Bacon turned to me. "What are you doing here?"

I stretched my spine to stand as tall as possible. "I've come to join your army."

"I have no army, not yet."

"But you will. When you get that commission, I'm coming with you."

"Are you a good shot?"

"For years I've helped keep meat on the table. But that's not why you need me."

"And why would I need *you?*"

A shadow rose like smoke before me, obscuring the glow of the fireplace. The shadow assumed Naokan's form. His face appeared first as a vague splotch, then solidified until I could see every stripe of his war paint. In my mind I lifted my pistol and fired . . .

"You need me as a spy."

"A spy?" His eyes narrowed. "What talent qualifies you to be a spy?"

"I speak Susquehannock."

Six

BACON SPRANG TO his feet and towered over me, his face dark, his eyes accusing. "Susquehannocks are murderers and thieves. How did you learn their language?"

"I'm a member of the tribe."

"You can't—"

"I am," I said, interrupting him. "Naokan, grandson of the medicine man—he'd been out hunting when he fell and wedged his foot between two logs. A bear was about to maul him when I came along and killed the bear. Afterward he made me his blood brother."

Brothers forever, Naokan had said.

Memories of our good times together poured through me like a summer flood: stalking game through the forest, building the canoe, teaching each other the names of plants and animals in our own tongues.

With those good memories came again the memory of Okahanah when he had growled: "All white men are bad. All white men must die." His face had twisted with anger because Naokan had dared to show me the location of their village.

"I told you yesterday, I know where their village is," I reminded Bacon now. "If they've moved it, I can track them."

Bacon's lips flared back from his teeth in a snarl that made me think of the raging bear when it had towered over Nahokan, claws ready for the death strike.

"Indians are savages," he said. "We'll kill them all or drive them out."

Presley snorted. "Can't do that without your army."

Bacon's fists clenched like mallets. "Berkeley loves Indians more than he loves Virginians."

"What he loves is the money he makes off the Indian beaver trade," Presley said. "Has to keep that young wife of his dressed in the latest English fashions."

"What is your answer?" I asked Bacon. "Am I in or out?"

Lawrence sidled forward. "Take this boy's offer, Nathaniel. You need all the help you can get."

Bacon threw him a sardonic look. "What help will you give me, Lawrence?"

The foxlike gleam once more flickered in Lawrence's eyes, belying the bland smile. "Advice. I'll give advice."

Bacon turned his back on Lawrence in obvious contempt. "Hansford, should we take this boy with us?"

Before Hansford could answer, I said, "If you don't take me, I'll follow you anyway. I'll move so silently you won't even know I'm there."

Lawrence laughed. "Nathaniel, you've got yourself an Indian scout." To me he said, "I'm shorthanded right now, so you can wait tables for me here until Berkeley signs the commission. There's a shed out by the stable where you can sleep."

But Berkeley did not sign the commission the next day, or the next, or the next. By the fourth day Bacon allowed his men to take one of the sloops and sail back upriver to be with their families in case of new attacks.

That night, near closing time, Lawrence sent me to the baker across town with an order for two dozen loaves of bread for the next day. On the way home I decided to practice my scouting skills. I took to the shadows, blending in with the bushes and moving in silence as Naokan had taught me.

"You are one with the snake, flowing through the grass," he had said. "You are one with the wind, flowing through the trees."

Now, when I heard low voices coming from an alley off to one side, I slithered closer until I could pick out the words.

" . . . sure that Bacon's men have left town?"

"Most of them. Hansford is still around."

"Good. We'll get him and Bacon both."

Major Hone's voice. I crept forward under cover of a wagon and some barrels. Soon I saw dark shapes that became the silhouettes of soldiers.

"Remember what Berkeley said," Hone went on. "It must look like a tavern brawl. Just make sure that Bacon ends up dead."

I wriggled quickly backward through the alley until I reached the safety of the shadows beyond. One with the wind, I flew through the town and slipped into the tavern through the back door. I found Bacon, Hansford, and the elder Mr. Bacon seated near the fireplace, flagons in hand. Lawrence hovered nearby.

I hurried across the room, pointing toward Bacon and Hansford. "You must get out of here. Hone and his soldiers are on their way to kill you. Berkeley's orders."

The older Mr. Bacon jumped to his feet. "That treacherous villain. Let God forgive *him!*"

Bacon stood and drew his sword in one fluid movement. "Let them come. I'm ready."

Rising at the same time, Hansford asked urgently, "How many soldiers?"

"At least ten. It's supposed to look like a tavern brawl."

"Horses, out back." Lawrence gestured in the direction of the stable. "Take them and go."

Bacon's face twisted into a savage mask. "Run away from Berkeley like a coward? No! This time I'll bring *him* to his knees."

"You don't stand a sinner's chance in Hell against ten soldiers," old Mr. Bacon said. "Leave. Now."

Bacon's eyes flashed blue fire. "Again you tell me to back down."

"You'll do us no good if you're dead."

"We need you alive," Lawrence added at the same time.

Bacon fixed Lawrence with a dangerous glare. "And why do *you* need me, Lawrence?"

Lawrence smiled. Again I thought of a fox, sly, cunning.

"I need you to bring down Berkeley and take his place as governor."

"With you in the background to give me 'advice'?"

"Of course. I've always wanted to rule this colony. I will do it through you."

For one moment I thought Bacon might strike Lawrence down. Then he laughed. "Lawrence, you're a devious scoundrel."

Lawrence shrugged. "It's my strongest virtue."

"Enough of this," Hansford cried, grabbing Bacon's arm. "Come on, we've got to get out of here."

"I'm coming with you," I said.

Bacon threw me a quick look. "To act as my spy?"

"Yes."

He hesitated and then nodded. "All right, let's go." We led the horses through the shadows away from the tavern until we reached the edge of town. Then, abandoning caution, we mounted and galloped into the darkness.

Seven

ONE WITH THE WIND, *one with the snake.*
I slipped through the forest, following Susquehannock sign—the scuff of a moccasin print in damp leaf mold, a broken twig. Steam rose from the forest floor around me, drawn by the hot August sun that streamed in shafts through the leafy canopy above.

My stomach tightened with nervous anticipation. At last, after weeks of delay, this could be the day that I'd find and kill Naokan.

The frustration of the past several weeks still lay heavily upon me. I remembered how, following our escape from Jamestown, I had expected to go at once after Naokan. Not so. Bacon had reassembled his army, six hundred strong, and marched us all back to Jamestown to wrest the commission from Berkeley at gunpoint.

I had watched in amazement while Berkeley and Bacon strutted back and forth in front of the State House like rival roosters in a hen yard, challenging each other.

"We *will* have our commission," Bacon had shouted.

"You'll have to shoot me first," Berkeley replied as he ripped open his clothes to bare his breast. "Before God, a fair mark. Shoot!"

"All we want is the commission," Bacon responded. "We have not come to harm you."

But his pistol, held at the ready, and the leveled guns of his men, said otherwise.

It was then that the councilmen intervened. Leaning from the windows of the State House, they shouted at Berkeley, "Give him his commission!"

With ill grace, Berkeley did so while reminding Bacon that a document signed under duress is invalid.

We then marched in triumph from Jamestown, and I thought, *Now* we will fight the Susquehannocks.

Wrong again. Instead, Bacon led his men against the Doegs and Occhaneechis, who had attacked several plantations while we were confronting Berkeley. I'd come across Naokan's old village at one point, but found it abandoned. Meanwhile, Bacon went after more Doegs.

Finally, when I'd almost given up hope, Bacon said to me, "See if you can find the Susquehannocks."

As I now slipped forward through the undergrowth I lifted my head to sniff the air. Woodsmoke tickled my nostrils, along with the smell of roasting venison. A faint murmur of voices drifted on the wind, too far away to distinguish words. Susquehannock voices? I moved closer, straining to pick up a familiar phrase.

A mosquito whined close to my left ear but didn't land, repelled, I suspected, by the salve I'd smeared over all areas of exposed skin, a mixture of bear fat, powdered bloodroot, charcoal, and blue clay. Susquehannock salve, a recipe I'd learned from Naokan.

"Faugh, you look and smell just like an Indian!" Bacon had exclaimed in disgust when I'd rubbed my body with the salve and then donned deerskin leggings, breechclout, and moccasins, taken from a Doeg village.

"A good thing," I'd replied. "Susquehannocks can scent a white man a mile away. Besides, this salve discourages insects. You should try it."

I came to the edge of an open glade. A faint swish of grass whispered in my ears and I dropped to my belly and slithered into a thicket. Despite the suffocating heat, my skin chilled when a Susquehannock warrior slid into view. Black war paint striped his face. His scalp, shaved on the right side to keep his hair from tangling in his bowstring, sported a tall bristling cockscomb that arched from the center of his brow over the top of his head and down toward the nape of his neck where the long hair from the other side of his head was tied with a leather thong that held two feathers, the mark of every Susquehannock warrior. He turned his face in my direction and I recognized, with a surge of shock, the thick brows and cruel mouth of Tano, who had been Okahanah's second-in-command. With Okahanah dead, Tano would now be war chief of Naokan's village.

Another warrior appeared behind Tano, and another, treading single file. For one heart-stopping moment I thought that Tano had seen me, but his gaze, usually as sharp as a cutlass, slid past the thicket, and I thanked whatever gods might be listening for the bear grease and charcoal that had darkened my skin to the color of dirt.

I counted, waiting tensely for Naokan to appear: six, seven, eight warriors, all wearing war paint. Five of them carried long bows and had quivers of arrows strapped to their backs. Three carried muskets. They flowed past, silent as smoke, and vanished into the forest beyond.

But no Naokan.

I remained motionless for several minutes, knowing that Tano's ears could pick up the footfall of a mouse on moss. At last I slithered from the thicket and scrambled away on all fours until I reached the cover of a stand of scrub oak. Then I rose and headed at a run toward Bacon's camp, four miles away. A protruding branch from a bramble bush glanced harmlessly off the buckskin leggings. My moccasined feet moved noiselessly over the leaf mold that carpeted the ground.

"Sturdy leather boots, that's what you need," Bacon had said when I'd put on the moccasins.

"Not so," I'd replied. "If you tramp through the forest in heavy boots, you'd might as well ring a bell to tell the Indians you're coming."

Sure enough, I now picked up the racket of Bacon's camp

long before I arrived: shouts and laughter, the rhythmical thud of an ax against wood. No wonder the Susquehannocks kept escaping our grasp.

I slipped into camp, avoiding the sentries, just to prove how lax our guard had become. Bacon didn't even know I was there until I suddenly stood before him. He jumped to his feet, hand on sword, before recognition cleared the grimace from his face.

"Zounds, boy, you'll get yourself killed if you aren't careful."

"And so will you. You should double the sentries and give them less ale."

Ignoring that, he asked, "What did you find?"

"Susquehannocks. The ones who killed my family. Four miles to the northwest."

His jaw tightened, his eyes kindled. "How many?"

"Two months ago the people in that band numbered around two hundred."

"Including the women and children?"

"Yes."

He nodded with satisfaction. "And some of the men will be too old to fight. That means no more than sixty, maybe seventy warriors, wouldn't you say?"

"Yes."

"Then we outnumber those warriors ten to one."

He beckoned toward someone behind me. I turned to see Hansford approaching, a big grin on his face.

"Robert!" He strode forward and clapped a hand on my shoulder. "Glad you made it back with your head intact. What—"

"He found Susquehannocks," Bacon interrupted brusquely. "We attack tomorrow."

"We attack today," I said. "The men I saw had war stripes on their faces. They were headed back to their camp for a feast. Venison. I smelled it cooking. They'll fill their bellies today and then they'll go marauding tomorrow. We should attack first, while we still have the advantage of surprise."

Bacon shook his head, a look of grudging admiration on his face. "Robert, you've got the makings of an officer."

I shrugged. "Common sense, that's all."

"Hansford, call the men—," Bacon began.

"You need to warn them," I interrupted. "Susquehannock warriors are fierce fighters, worse than any we have faced so far. They can throw a hatchet or shoot an arrow with the accuracy of a bullet, and almost as fast. Some of them have guns, as well."

Bacon's face darkened like a storm cloud. "Guns! That damned Berkeley, trading guns to the Indians for beaver skins!"

"He denies that," Hansford pointed out.

"Of course he denies it, but it's true. Someday, after we've pushed out the Indians, we will march back to Jamestown and—" He broke off and stared into air, a speculative look in his eyes. After a moment he turned back to us, his face once more fired with the fierce determination that I'd seen before each battle.

"Berkeley will have to wait for now," he said. "Today we fight the Susquehannocks."

Excitement coursed down my spine. I would shoot Naokan at close range. He would recognize me before I killed him. My brother. Now my enemy.

Pomanah's face rose before me, her eyes as soft and dark as a doe's.

"Kill only the warriors," I said. "The women and children can do us no harm."

"Did the Susquehannocks spare your mother, brother, and sister?" Bacon asked.

Again I saw the red-trimmed arrow protruding from my mother's back, saw the broken bodies of Mary and Charlie.

"No," I whispered.

Bacon nodded as if no more needed to be said.

"Call the men," he told Hansford. "Tell them we march in an hour."

Eight

DESPITE MY WARNING about keeping quiet, Bacon's soldiers crashed through the forest like stampeding horses, breaking the limbs of trees as they passed, snapping twigs under their feet. The supply cart, carrying, among other things, two kegs of black powder, creaked and groaned over the rough ground as the horses leaned into their traces.

When we reached the area at last, Bacon sent me forward to scout the scene. Just as I expected, the village lay empty in the golden slant of late afternoon light. I inhaled the smoke from the still-smoldering cook fires while my skin prickled with premonition. I knew the Susquehannock warriors too well to think that they had fled. When they'd heard our approach, they had hidden the women and children away from the village and were now waiting in ambush. Clutching my pistol, I slithered backward through the brush to give Bacon the news.

"Aieee!"

"Yi hiii!"

The savage yelps of the warriors, surging from all directions, rent the air like bolts of lightning. I rose to my feet and ran toward Bacon's soldiers, dodging this way and that to foil the whistling flight of arrows. A bullet thudded into a tree near my head. A second bullet grazed my shoulder, searing the skin as if I had been touched by a burning stick. I dropped to my belly in the grass.

"Got one!" shouted a voice in English.

My stomach cramped when I realized I'd been mistaken for a Susquehannock. I scrambled into a thicket and crouched low, listening to the thud of approaching boots. A probing musket swept aside the bushes and I looked into the battle-fevered eyes of Darrow, one of Bacon's men.

Thwack.

Darrow's body jerked and his face stiffened with surprise. His fingers clenched, the gun jumped and a bullet exploded into the dirt near my left arm. Then he collapsed on top of me, the arrow protruding from his back.

I shoved his body aside and jumped up, running once more in the direction of Bacon's men while yelling, "It's me, it's Robert!"

The tumult of shouts and gunfire swallowed my cries. Another bullet whined past my ear. Then an explosion, loud as a crack of thunder, shook the forest, lifting a cloud of dust.

Oh, God, the powder blew up, I thought.

I dived into the bushes as pebbles and sticks rained down like hail. I kept crawling, unsure, now, in what direction I was headed. An acrid smell scorched the air, burning my lungs. As I slithered over a broken wheel from the cart, I found myself looking directly into two dark eyes in a dark-skinned face, barely visible in the shadows. A Susquehannock. My heart constricted with rage. I lifted my pistol and aimed it between those eyes.

"Brother!"

The cry, desperate and demanding, pierced the sound of battle. My breath pushed from my lungs. My arms weakened and dropped, lowering the gun.

"Pomanah?"

"Naokan—he's hurt."

She shoved aside some leaves. Naokan lay unmoving, arms flung wide, legs sprawled, his face streaked with blood. Gorge rose in my throat. There he was at last, my enemy, the one who had killed my family. This time my arms did not waver as I lifted the pistol and aimed at his heart.

"No!" Pomanah flung herself forward, covering his body with hers.

"Move."

She turned her head and held my eyes with hers. "He did not kill your family."

"His arrows——"

"Naokan tried to stop the war party that day. It made Okahanah angry. He stripped away Naokan's feathers, cut his hair, and took his arrows. Naokan was not there when your family died."

She stared at me unwavering and I read on her face the truth of her words.

Naokan had told me many times how a warrior who defied the war chief stood disgraced before his people. He lost his weapons, lost his right to hunt or fight as a man. Instead, he was made to cook, chew hides for moccasins, gather wood with the women.

I leaned forward and saw that Naokan's tall cockscomb, the pride of all warriors, was indeed gone, as was the rest of his hair. Short tufts now bristled about his head like pine needles. Blood welled from the angry wound that had laid open his scalp; burns blistered his forehead, the skin around his eyes. When he stirred and moaned, Pomanah sat up at once and cradled his face in her hands.

"Was he near the cart when it blew up?" I asked.

She nodded. "Tano left me in the village. Naokan came back to find me."

Naokan moaned again and lifted one hand toward his head. Pomanah reached out and grabbed his hand before he could touch the wound. His eyes slitted open. I waited for him to say my name, but his eyes remained unfocused, holding no expression. I raised my hand and passed it back and forth in front of his face. He did not respond to the movement. Pomanah looked at me in alarm. She, too, lifted fingers to wave them before his staring eyes. Still he did not respond. As I watched, the stone of hatred I had carried for so long dissolved into dust.

Naokan, my enemy . . . my brother . . . was blind.

Nine

I HAD WANTED NAOKAN'S death with a passion
that seared my soul. Now, looking at his damaged face, his
ruined eyes, his shorn hair, I wanted him well, wanted the
flow of time to run backward to those days when we had
hunted together and learned each other's words.

I scrambled into the thicket beside Pomanah and shook
the branches back into place behind me to shield us from the
soldiers' eyes. The repeated bark of musket fire bounced off
the trees around us while the acrid smell of the exploded
powder kegs still soiled the air, along with screams and
curses.

I held my pistol ready, wondering what I would do if we
were found. Could I shoot a fellow Virginian, a man like my
own father who was fighting to keep his family safe? On the
other hand, could I kill a Susquehannock in the presence of
Naokan and Pomanah, kill a member of their village?

I glanced toward Pomanah. She returned my look, her
face filled with trust. I silently cursed both Bacon and
Okahanah for the war that raged around us.

If we could just wait it out until the fighting ceased and
the soldiers went away, maybe we could find a safe place
where Pomanah could nurse Naokan back to health and
sight. And then . . .

My mind searched frantically for answers.

Then . . . what? Was there someplace where the three of
us could live together, make our own world? What about my
plantation? Could we slip back there, build a lodge from
saplings and grass mats?

Pomanah turned her head sharply toward the right. Then

I heard it, too, the thud of several sets of boots running toward us, heavy leather boots that crunched twigs, kicked up leaves and stones, unlike moccasins that whispered over a path like the sigh of wind.

Pomanah placed her fingers against Naokan's lips. I hoped he was awake enough to know the meaning of her gesture.

"Captain Hastings killed their war chief!" shouted a voice in triumph.

Cheers greeted the announcement.

"What about prisoners?"

"Bacon says no prisoners."

"Did you see the way that woman attacked me with her teeth and hands after I shot her baby? Just like a wild animal, not even human."

Pomanah's face remained as impassive as a rock. Naokan shifted slightly, turning his head toward the sound of the voices. From the stiffening of his body, the clenching of his fists, I knew he had understood what was said. The thud of boots grew closer. I checked my pistol to make sure it was primed and ready. The soldiers drew level and pounded past, stirring the leaves around us. Only as their steps faded with distance did I relax. Could I really have shot them if they had discovered us? I still didn't know.

We waited in silence as the sound of the battle surged, diminished, surged again. At last the shots grew fewer in number and finally ceased altogether.

"It's over!" shouted someone in the distance. "We got most of them. The rest have fled."

More cheers, as if they had just won a game.

The thud of boots approached again, striding purposefully.

"Hansford?" Bacon's voice, loud and authoritative.

"I've found Darrow," Hansford called from some distance away. "He's dead."

"Hell's gate!" Bacon's oath exploded like a musket shot. I

peered through the leaves to see Bacon standing nearby, pistol in hand. Another planter strode toward him, a big man who wore a tartan sash as a baldric.

"Did you hear that?" Bacon asked the man. "Darrow's dead."

I recognized the man then: William Drummond, a Scotsman who had once served as governor of the Carolinas before moving to Virginia.

Drummond swept his hat from his head and rubbed his forehead with his sleeve. "Poor Darrow. The Indians murdered his wife and children, and now they've killed him, too."

Images of brown children, white children, Mary, Charlie, danced in my mind like leaves caught in a whirlwind. The children laughed, sang, tagged each other in play. Then their faces changed. Blood flowered their clothes and they fell to earth.

Enough, I cried in silence. *Enough*.

Bacon pivoted, scanning the area. His gaze passed over our thicket, paused, returned, and I saw his eyes narrow. As he strode forward I jumped to my feet.

"General!" I called.

I crashed from the thicket, hoping to distract him before he noticed Naokan and Pomanah. Undeterred, he stepped around me and shoved the branches aside. Naokan rose on his elbows, his eyes still blank as he turned his face toward the noise. Pomanah crouched beside him like a startled fawn. Bacon lifted his pistol.

"No!" Leaping forward, I grabbed Bacon's wrist and turned the gun to one side. "These are my prisoners."

"No prisoners," he growled.

"I know these two," I said, still holding his wrist as if in a vise. "The girl is a healer. She can doctor our wounded."

"Keep her, then. This one dies." He jerked his chin toward Naokan while struggling to free his arm from my grip.

"He knows where other Susquehannock villages lie. Keep him alive for now so I can question him," I insisted.

Bacon shook his head. "It's dangerous to keep him alive."

"Look at him." I turned and pointed, forcing scorn into my voice. "He can't see. What harm can he do?"

For the first time I slid my gaze toward Pomanah, willing her to understand what I was trying to do. Her face had frozen into an expressionless mask.

"Can he walk?" Bacon asked.

"Stand up!" I barked in Susquehannock. "Both of you, stand up."

To my relief Naokan struggled upright. When he swayed, Pomanah rose quickly and grabbed his arm.

"Go along with this," I growled, still speaking Susquehannock as I stepped forward to shake my fist toward Pomanah in a threatening way. "Do not let them know you understand English."

For one brief moment her eyes flickered, but her face revealed no emotion.

Hansford hurried forward to join us.

"What's going on?" he asked.

Bacon glanced toward me, his face hard. "Robert wants to take these two as prisoners."

"For now," I said. "Later . . ." I shrugged, pretending I did not care what came later.

Hansford's brows drew together as he considered the proposal. "You know, Nathaniel, that's not a bad idea. If we display Susquehannock prisoners on our march back to Jamestown, it might inspire other planters to join us."

Surprise needled my skin. "We're marching back to Jamestown?"

Bacon nodded, his face grim. "Berkeley has withdrawn the commission and once more named us rebels. Now that we've won this victory, Berkeley will have to back down."

An idea budded in my mind and blossomed into a plan. Gesturing toward Naokan and Pomanah, I said, "Hansford is right, we can use these two to win support for you. We'll paint war stripes on their faces, stick feathers in their hair, make them look like savages."

"They *are* savages. They'll cut our throats if we aren't careful." Bacon turned toward Drummond. "Guard these two. Shoot them if they make a wrong move."

"He'll do it, so take care," I warned Pomanah, once more speaking the Susquehannock words in a harsh voice. "As soon as Naokan can see again, I'll help you both escape."

Could Pomanah really heal Naokan? I did not know. But I did know this: A blind warrior could not survive long in the forest, even with help.

Please, make him well, I begged in silence, and realized my plea was a prayer.

Would God honor a prayer for a heathen? That was another question to which I did not know the answer.

Ten

IT'S A WONDER to me that armies get anything done. When you take hundreds of soldiers into a forest and try to feed them and doctor them and move them around in some kind of organized way, it's like trying to herd fish in the ocean. Despite Bacon's plans to march again on Jamestown, it took us over a week to get ready. We buried our dead and transported our injured men to various plantations in the area where they could be treated. We baked corn cakes and roasted venison to feed us on the march.

I was kept so busy that I had little chance to see Naokan and Pomanah, who were placed in a prison tent under close guard. Sometimes Bacon did allow Pomanah, still guarded, to gather roots and leaves in the forest to make medicine for the injured soldiers, and on those days I did contrive to speak with her, but our encounters were brief, just a word or two from her to let me know that Naokan still could not see.

One afternoon during a heavy downpour, which had caused most of the men in camp to seek cover, I slogged through the mud to the prison tent.

"I've come to question them," I told the guard.

He shrugged, looking miserable as rain poured from the brim of his hat onto his shoulders. I knelt and crawled through the flap into the dimness. Puddles covered the floor where rain had leaked through the rents in the canvas.

"Robert," Pomanah whispered.

Naokan, his eyes shielded by bandages, sat up and extended his right arm. I slid forward and grasped his arm just below the elbow, laying my arm against his in the

Susquehannock sign of friendship. As his fingers closed around my arm, I asked, "Are you better?"

"Yes," he said, but Pomanah, her face filled with worry, shook her head.

I held Pomanah's eyes with mine to let her know I understood. To Naokan I said, "Good, my brother. A few more days and you'll be fine."

Naokan released my arm and sat back. "Then we will hunt again."

I could tell he knew just as well as I did that it might not be true.

Pomanah leaned forward and gently touched the scab on my shoulder where the bullet had grazed my skin.

"Almost healed," I said. "That salve you made took care of it. And that soldier you treated yesterday for fever, he's doing better, too."

"When does your war chief—?" she began.

"He says we leave for Jamestown tomorrow if the rain stops."

Naokan's jaw tightened. "He will not need us after we reach the white men's town. Is that when we die?"

I'd wondered the same thing.

"Just as soon as you can see, I'll help you escape. We'll look for your people who got away—"

Naokan shook his head. "They will not take me back. I defied our war chief. Now he is dead and our village is gone."

Guilt twisted my stomach. Naokan's village was gone because I'd shown Bacon where it was. I swallowed gall when I recalled how Bacon's men had piled the bodies of the dead Susquehannocks inside the lodges in the village and then set them ablaze.

"They will accept Pomanah," Naokan continued. "Leave me here and go with—"

"No," Pomanah said.

"She's right," I told Naokan. "When it's time to leave, I'm coming with you. The three of us can—"

"I would hold you back. I cannot hunt. I cannot scout. You'd have to lead me." There was no self-pity in Naokan's voice, just a flat statement of fact.

"You *will* see again!" I said firmly. "And then . . . what about other villages? Would they take you in? What about Susquehannocks to the north?"

Naokan shook his head. "They would not want a warrior who has defied his war chief. They are fighting now with the Senecas—"

But I knew that, of course. Not long after we had first become friends, Naokan had told me about the fierce inter-tribal war that was raging to the north and how his people had been chased out of their territory and down into Virginia by rival tribes.

A dark cloud fogged my spirit when I thought of Indians murdering each other and massacring colonists, colonists murdering Indians and fighting among themselves.

And it wasn't only here, it was overseas, as well. My father had told me how cousins continued to kill each other there, English, Irish, Scots, bloody slaughter on all sides, often in the name of God.

"Robert? Are you in there?"

Bacon's voice.

I signaled farewell to Pomanah and scrambled out into the rain. Rising, I gave Bacon a sharp salute.

"Just questioning the prisoners, Sir."

He grinned. "You sound like a soldier, Robert, but you don't look like one."

I glanced down at my breechclout and leggings, stained with mud and rain.

"You can't dress like an Indian on our march to Jamestown. You'll have to wear regular clothes."

"Yes, Sir."

He wrinkled his nose in a grimace of disgust. "And for God's sake wash off that bear grease. You smell bad enough when the sun is out, but you stink even worse when you're wet."

"But—"

"I know, I know, you think mosquitoes carry fever and the salve keeps the mosquitoes away."

"The Susquehannocks believe it, and they've lived in the forest longer than we have."

He coughed, a deep racking cough, as he scratched the back of one hand. "The mosquitoes *are* bad this year."

"Yes."

"Hansford and I are having a conference and we need to ask you some questions." He sniffed the air again. "If we can stand to be near you."

He turned and slogged away through the mud. I followed, not pleased at the prospect of having to wear white men's clothes again. Wool breeches, wool stockings, heavy boots.

We arrived at the lean-to, which Bacon's men had built for him under the protection of the trees. Hansford huddled inside on a log, coat collar drawn up around his ears.

"Miserable weather, Robert," he said, throwing me a grin.

I nodded, feeling certain that he and Bacon had not brought me here to discuss the rain. Bacon entered the lean-to and sat down on the other end of the log. I crouched inside the entrance, waiting for them to reveal their purpose. Bacon stared at me fixedly for a long moment, and I began to fear he'd guessed I was planning to help Naokan and Pomanah escape. My thoughts raced as I tried to come up with some argument for keeping them alive. When Bacon opened his mouth at last, I tensed, still searching for an answer.

"Robert, how do you feel about England?"

His question surprised me so much that I blinked and sat

back on my heels. "I don't know. I've never been to England."

"What about the king? How do you feel about him?"

"I've never seen the king."

"You've *heard* about the king," Bacon insisted. "What have you heard?"

Was this a trick? I eyed them both warily. "I've heard he is a conceited fop who doesn't give a damn for anyone but himself."

Bacon impaled me with a sharp look. "Are you an Englishman?"

"No, I'm a Virginian."

A fierce gleam filled Bacon's face as if a torch had been ignited inside his body. "There, Hansford. The voice of the new generation. Virginians. Not Englishmen."

Hansford shook his head. "I don't know, Nathaniel. Fighting Berkeley is one thing. Fighting the king is another."

"We could win, I know we could. King Charles is too busy sparring with the Dutch to bother about Virginia."

"If he should decide to send troops—"

"How many could he send? He's spread too thin already."

"But Berkeley—"

"— is an old man living in the past. I tell you, Hansford, the time is right. We already have our army. People here are angry with England because of the taxes and the trade restrictions—"

"You're not talking about rebellion now, Nathaniel, you're talking about revolution."

"That's exactly what I'm talking about."

Oh, no, I thought, *an all-out war.*

Again the images of dying brown and white children spun in my mind.

Bacon pulled a sheet of paper from his coat. "I've drawn up an oath of allegiance for the men to sign. I want the two of you to have the honor of putting your names first, just under mine."

Hansford took the paper and scanned it. "Nathaniel, this is dangerous."

"It merely asserts our rights."

"It goes further than that, and you know it. Here, where it says we will follow you against the king's troops if the time comes . . . people aren't ready for this."

"I say they are. All they need is for someone to lead them, to show them the way."

The fire in Bacon's eyes, the fervor in his voice, held me spellbound even while a warning voice in my head whispered, *This spells trouble.*

"I have ink and a quill," Bacon said. He pointed toward a table made from a stump. Sitting on the stump was a clay pot that held a long stiff feather. "Which of you wants to sign first?"

It was obvious that he expected us to comply. When neither of us moved, he fixed me with the glare of a hawk.

"Robert, what happened to your father in England?"

"He was deported. You know that."

"For theft. Was he innocent or guilty?"

"He was innocent."

"Yet he wore the brand of a thief."

"Yes."

Joanna's voice echoed through my mind, telling me once more of her arrest and deportation for stealing the chicken to feed her dying child. Her face appeared before me, haggard and worn. I looked again into her pain-filled eyes.

Bacon turned to Hansford. "Did you get a good price for your tobacco last year?"

"You know I didn't."

"Why?"

"Because the king's taxes took all my profits."

Bacon nodded. "Could you have gotten a good price from the Dutch?"

"Yes, of course. But the trade restrictions—"

"Imposed by the king."

Hansford shook his head, a look of desperation twisting his face. "Nathaniel, we've been through all this before. Yes, we'd be better off without England. Yes, we'd do better on our own. But—"

Nathaniel turned once more to me. "Robert, *you* . . . you and others like you . . . are the future of Virginia. Do you want to kneel to a King who doesn't give a fig for you or do you want to stand on your own?"

He radiated a power that I could not resist. When he held out the paper I took it.

"Robert—" Hansford began in a warning tone.

Right at that moment I hated the king. I hated him for the brand on my father's hand, for the grief in Joanna's eyes.

"All right, I'll sign."

I placed the paper on the stump, knelt in the dirt, took the quill, and firmly wrote my name below Bacon's.

"Hansford?" Bacon demanded.

Their eyes locked.

"Hansford, I need you," Bacon said in a softer tone. "Yours is a name the people respect."

The two men regarded each other for a long moment in silence. At last Hansford took the quill from me and wrote his name next to mine.

"Good," Bacon said. "You won't regret this."

I could tell from the set of Hansford's jaw, the furrow between his brows, that he already regretted it.

Eleven

THE NEXT MORNING dawned bright and clear. In a ringing speech Bacon praised the men for their courage in battle and exhorted them to stand firm against Berkeley in asserting their rights. Several times he used the phrase, "We, the people of Virginia."

He did not actually mention revolution, but I could read the meaning that underlay his words. At one point I caught Hansford's eye. He gave me a bleak look before turning away.

During the night, away from the power of Bacon's personality, I'd decided I wanted nothing to do with a war against England, but I knew that if I stayed with him I would get pulled into that war as surely as a leaf gets caught up by the wind.

And Naokan and Pomanah—what would happen to them?

We could wait no longer for Naokan to heal; we had to escape. With my hunting skills I could keep us fed, at least for a while. And if . . . *when* Naokan could see again, we would hunt together. We'd set up our own village, just the three of us, somewhere in the mountains to the west.

Cursing the heavy boots that sheathed my legs in lead, the wool breeches and rough linen shirt that scratched my skin, I slipped away from the gathering and hurried to the prison tent. Perhaps in all the excitement of the morning, Bacon had forgotten to post a guard.

Wrong. He had increased the guard to four men. Pomanah and Naokan, mouths pulled into tight lines, stood in silence before the tent as one of the men used a stick of charcoal to draw stripes on their cheeks and chins. Someone had already pinned turkey feathers in Pomanah's hair and stuck other feathers in the top edge of the bandage that still surrounded Naokan's head and eyes. Pomanah's short buckskin dress, stained from days of constant wear, hung about her slender body like a rag, while her moccasins were clumps of mud. Naokan's moccasins and breechclout had fared no better. The two of them did indeed look savage, little better than beasts.

The man with the charcoal glanced toward me and grinned. "What do you think? Will this put the fear of God into Berkeley?"

I forced a grin in response. "It certainly puts the fear of God into me."

Another man stepped forward and knelt to snap iron bracelets connected by chains around Naokan's ankles. Then he did the same thing to Pomanah. The sound of those locks clicking shut struck me like a physical blow.

"Who ordered—"

"General Bacon. He doesn't want these two trying to escape before we reach Jamestown. He plans to put them on display there, along with Berkeley."

Anger surged through me like a hot wind. "Good idea," I said, still grinning. "Maybe you should throw away the key."

I stared hard at him, willing him to toss the key into the bushes where I could retrieve it later.

"Bacon wants it back."

"I'll take it to him."

The man's eyes grew hard and his jaw clenched. "He pledged me to bring it back to him in person."

Silently cursing the man's stubborness, I said in Susquehannock, "Don't worry, I'll free you as soon as I can."

"What are you saying?" the man with the key asked me, his face dark with suspicion.

"I'm telling them they'd better not try to escape."

The man continued to frown. "If they do try, Bacon has ordered us to kill them. He says Susquehannocks are as dangerous as snakes."

I nodded. "He's right."

From the direction of the gathering there rose a chorus of cheers. The man with the charcoal straightened and glanced in that direction.

"Sounds as if Bacon has finished his speech," he said. "We'd better get this tent down and packed for the trip."

"My medicines," Pomanah murmured in Susquehannock.

I entered the tent and retrieved the leather pouch that held her leaves and roots.

One of the other men grunted his approval. "She may be a wild one, but that poultice she made drew the poison from the carbuncle I had on my neck."

I moved closer to peer at Naokan's face, noting that the blisters were gone from his cheeks and the skin there seemed to be healing. A pungeant odor wafted from the bandages. Afraid that I was revealing too much concern, I waved my hand in front of my nose and said to the man with the carbuncle, "Faugh! Did your poultice stink as bad as that?"

He snorted. "Damn near."

Several soldiers hurried toward us, their faces flushed, their voices excited. "Bacon is right, we're Virginians, not Englishmen," one of them said.

"Berkeley is too old and lives in the past. It's Bacon who should head up this colony," said another.

The guard with the key stepped out to meet them. "Are we ready to march?"

"Yes."

"Tell them to move," the guard said to me while pointing at Naokan and Pomanah. "And tell them they'd better not fall behind."

Making the Susquehannock words sound harsh and angry, I said, "I'll set you free if it's the last thing I do."

I walked ahead of them to kick the stones and fallen branches out of their way as we headed for Jamestown.

Twelve

THE CLOSER WE drew to Jamestown the more our ranks increased. Planters left their homes, their fields, to join us, and brought their servants along The fever of rebellion filled the air, as catching as the fever that drifted from the river marshes. Even women joined the march, some of them respectable wives in dresses made of silk, some of them harlots in rough cotton skirts, their bodices loosely laced.

One of the women who joined us was Sarah Drummond, wife of William Drummond. A sturdy woman with intense blue eyes, she proved to be as hot a firebrand as Bacon himself.

One day she picked up a stick and broke it in two, declaring, "I care no more for the power of England than for this broken straw."

Drummond stepped forward to join her, proclaiming, "We're in over our shoes. We might as well be in over our boots."

Some people argued at first against so radical an attitude. Then came word that the Appomattox Indians had joined the Doegs in an attack against two plantations to the north and that Berkeley had provided no defense.

We'd reached Middle Plantation by then, just a few miles from Jamestown. Bacon left us camped there under the command of Hansford and Drummond while he took a select band of soldiers to pursue and destroy those attackers. He was gone for a number of days, which caused uneasiness in the camp, but when at last he returned triumphant to give another of his inflammatory speeches, his followers reacted with cheers and enthusiasm. Many of those who had resisted signing the oath of allegiance now crowded forward to do so.

Taking advantage of the tumult, I sought out Naokan and Pomanah, who stood under guard to one side. My breath caught in my throat when I saw that Naokan's bandages had been removed.

"What—?" I began.

Naokan kept his face expressionless, but the flicker of recognition I saw in his eyes gave me the answer.

"Oh, my God!" I exclaimed in English and then remembered to switch to Susquehannock. "You can see."

"Shapes. Shadows."

"When did you first notice—"

"Yesterday," Pomanah said.

Naokan took it up. "Yesterday I saw light. Today I see you."

My heart surged with excitement. "We'll escape and head toward the mountains to the west—"

"Not in these."

Naokan indicated the shackles on his and Pomanah's ankles. The flesh on either side of those circles of iron oozed blood and matter where the metal had roughed away the skin.

"Time to get the key," I said.

I headed for the house that Bacon had commandeered as his headquarters. When I arrived at the front door, I found Edward Cheesman, a planter from upriver, standing guard duty.

"Private business for General Bacon," I said briskly.

He grinned. "Spying on Indians in there, are you, Robert?"

I dropped my officious manner and grinned back. "I hear that a band of Susquehannocks slipped through the back door while you were taking a nap."

"In that case you'd better look," he said as he stepped aside.

I hurried through the open doorway and entered the library, which was just to the left of the front hall. In three strides I crossed the carpet to Bacon's desk and shuffled through the papers there. Finding no key on top of the desk, I rifled the drawers, one by one. Still no key. Bacon's coat hung from a peg on a coatrack to one side. I had just finished going through the pockets without any luck when I heard Bacon's voice greet Cheesman at the door. Stepping to a window, I pretended to examine the view.

"Robert! I was just looking for you!"

I turned as Bacon, accompanied by Hansford and Drummond, strode into the room.

"There was such a crowd I decided to wait here for you," I said. "Congratulations on your victory."

Bacon's eyes burned with a fanatical fire. "Soon we will have killed all the Indians in Virginia or driven them from our borders. No one can stand in our way, not now."

"Not even the king," put in Drummond, his craggy face hard with resolve.

Hansford shook his head. "We have to conquer Berkeley first."

"So we do," said Bacon. Turning once more to me, he said, "Robert, that's why I was looking for you. I want you to slip into Jamestown tonight and bring back a report on the number of troops and the kinds of weapons Berkeley has amassed, any new defenses he may have built."

"Yes, Sir."

"Nathaniel, if he gets caught—" Hansford began.

"He won't get caught. He's as wily as any Indian, you know that."

"Sir, speaking of Indians . . ." I paused, letting the sentence hang while I gathered my words.

"Yes?"

"Those shackles around the ankles of the Susquehannock prisoners—they're wearing away the skin and causing sores. Can I take the shackles off just long enough for the girl to apply a salve?"

Bacon frowned. "Those are the people who killed your family. Why should you care how they feel?"

"I don't, but you said you wanted to display them, along with Berkeley, after you capture Jamestown. They can't march if they're crippled, so I thought some salve—"

"They can walk as far as Jamestown, even with those sores. After that, it doesn't matter."

The finality with which he made that statement chilled my blood.

"And then?" I probed, although I already knew the answer. This man who killed all Indians without compunction would see no reason to spare two Susquehannocks, the most savage, in his opinion, of all his enemies.

"They will have served their purpose," he replied in a flat voice. "Besides, even if I wished to do so I could not remove their shackles. I've lost the key."

My thoughts were mice, searching in despair for a way out of the trap. That's when I remembered Josiah Wheeler, the Jamestown blacksmith. He would have tools— a hammer, a chisel—that I might use to break the locks on the shackles. If I could steal those tools and lug them back to Bacon's camp . . .

"I'll leave now and have the information for you by morning," I said.

Bacon clapped me on the shoulder. "Robert, you're a good soldier and a good Indian fighter. Your father would be proud."

My father. The Susquehannocks had murdered him, yet here I was, plotting against my own people to save two members of that tribe.

My father had often said to me as I was growing up, "Keep your integrity, Robert. Always do what is right."

If he were here, what would he advise? That I stay with Bacon's army? Fight England? Betray Naokan and Pomanah?

I no longer knew what was right, but I knew what I had to do. Turning my back on Bacon, I strode from the room.

Thirteen

ONE WITH THE snake, I slithered through the grass in the deepening twilight, hoping that the shadows would hide me from the probing eyes of Berkeley's guards who patrolled the ramparts of a log and earthen wall that now shielded Jamestown from a land attack. I could see at once that a charge across the expanse of open land that lay between the neck of the peninsula and the ramparts would be suicide. Bacon would need a breastwork of his own in order to bring his men within striking distance of the wall if his assault on Jamestown were to succeed.

I wriggled closer, struggling to make sense out of the occasional words that floated toward me on the errant wind.

"—a thousand men."

My skin chilled. Were they speaking of Berkeley's troops? Bacon's forces numbered far fewer than a thousand, even if one counted slaves and indentureds who had either run away to join Bacon's cause or had been brought into the fray when their masters joined Bacon's army.

". . . when the king's men arrive."

My stomach knotted. That meant that Berkeley had indeed sent to England for reinforcements. How long ago? I thought back to the several ships that had sailed toward England with cargos of tobacco during the summer. Plenty of time had gone by for some of those ships to have reached England and begun their return voyage with a cargo of king's troops. Perhaps some of the troops had already arrived. A thousand men? If so, then entering the town would be more dangerous than I'd thought. Maybe I should give up the idea—

Coward. I struck the ground with one clenched fist, cursing myself for that moment of weakness. I had come to get tools to set Naokan and Pomanah free, and for that I had to enter the town.

I crawled into a dip in the damp, spongy meadow. The grasses were thicker there, taller, intermixed with rushes. More snatches of conversation reached me as I edged toward the woods.

". . . women taken to safety."

"Berkeley . . . Cavalier of the old school. Women must be protected."

I reached a thicket and scrambled forward on hands and knees into a nearby grove of trees, grateful that I'd worn moccasins instead of heavy boots. Rising, I made my way through the underbrush to the river. Over a mile wide at that point, it rolled past in sluggish silence, slate gray beneath the darkening, star-sprinkled sky.

I found a log that was big enough to support my weight in the water, then slipped my hunting knife from the belt of my breeches and sawed several limbs from the log to make it more maneuverable. When the log was ready, I dragged it into the current, glad that I had left my pistol and powder horn behind in Bacon's camp. Keeping most of my body submerged, I hung on to the log and let it carry me downriver past the barricade.

Noises carry even better over water than over land, particularly on an evening when the air is still. The closer I got to the town, the more things I heard: the creaking of boats in the harbor as they rocked on the current, the shouts of men calling to each other along the shore, the clop of horses' hooves, the ring of a hammer on iron. When I drifted past a long boat with a night fisherman casting his line, I edged around to the back of the log, still hanging on, and submerged until just my nose was sticking out of the water.

My plan was to put into shore a little distance down the peninsula below Jamestown and make my way back to the cover of Aunt Charlotte's property. This proved to be surprisingly easy. The sentries were spaced so far apart that I wriggled past without any problem. Still, my heart sped up and my breath quickened when I approached the storage shed behind Aunt Charlotte's kitchen. Aware that Berkeley might have quartered troops in every home, I carefully edged closer, watching for lamplight in the windows of the big house. My breathing eased when I saw that the windows were dark. No noises came from inside the kitchen, no smell of food hung in the air. I decided that Berkeley had indeed sent the women to safety and that my aunt had taken Joanna and Amos with her.

My stomach rumbled. Remembering the crusty loaf of bread I had eaten in that kitchen back in June, I crept around to the kitchen door, hoping that Joanna might have left some cheese on a shelf or perhaps a basket of apples. At my touch the door creaked open, revealing the black maw of the room beyond.

I had not yet entered when I heard footsteps on the path behind me. Before I could whirl around, a hand clamped down on my shoulder and a knife probed my ribs.

"Who are you?" demanded a deep voice. "What do you want?"

For a moment I froze. Then the voice registered in my mind and I whispered, "Amos?"

The grip on my shoulder slackened slightly. "Who—?"

"Robert."

He removed the knife and spun me around. I could barely see his form in the darkness. "Where did you come from?"

"The river."

"What are you doing here?"

"Looking for something to eat."

"Come with me."

He led the way to his cabin near the stables. Once we were inside I saw that a few live coals flickered in the fireplace, which filled the center of one wall. Blankets draped the two small windows in the room, holding out the darkness, hiding the light inside.

Amos closed and latched the door behind us while motioning to a stool near the fireplace. Despite the warm evening I felt chilled in my wet clothes and so I leaned forward, welcoming the heat from the coals.

"Where is Aunt Charlotte?" I asked.

Amos tossed some kindling into the fireplace. As the kindling caught, he repositioned a small iron pot, which hung from the arm of a tall firedog, to bring it closer to the flames.

"The mistress and Joanna Berkeley sent them out of town," he said.

As always, I was struck by his rhythmical accent and by the intelligence that burned in the dark depths of his eyes.

"Berkeley sent the other women away, too," he went on. "To Greenspring, that's what the mistress said. For safety."

I stiffened in surprise. "But that's the governor's plantation! It's close to where Bacon is now camped."

He gave me a shrewd look. "You are still with Bacon?"

I did not answer that. Instead, I asked, "Why didn't you go with my aunt?"

"She left me here to guard the house and feed the chickens." His face was an ebony mask, its angles sharply defined by the growing flicker of flame. "I hear slaves have joined Bacon's army."

"They have. Indentureds, too."

"I hear Bacon wants to make his own country without England."

"I hear that, too."

"Will he free the slaves?"

He deserved the truth. "Amos, I don't know. He owns a large plantation—"

"With many slaves?"

I nodded.

He sat for a moment, absorbing that information. "He will not set us free."

"He's a strange man with a good side and a bad side. I don't know how he feels about slaves, but I do know he hates Indians."

Worry sat upon my shoulder, a heavy weight. "Look, Amos, I need to know, have the king's troops arrived?"

"Not yet. They will come, the mistress said. Berkeley sent his wife to England with letters for the king."

"How long ago?"

"Many weeks."

"How many men does Berkeley have here in Jamestown?"

"At least three hundred, maybe more." He gave me a long look of appraisal. "You swam past the guards to spy on the town."

I returned his look. "I'm also here for another reason. Two friends of mine—Bacon has taken them prisoner and locked them in chains. I need tools to set them free." I paused, then added, "They are Susquehannocks."

"The Susquehannocks killed your family."

"Naokan is my brother."

The nobility of Amos's bearing supported his claim that he had once been a king. "This is not unknown to me, this taking of an enemy as a brother. Was there a blood ceremony?"

"Yes." I held up my arm to show him the scar. "I've come to steal a hammer and chisel from the blacksmith."

"I will give you the tools."

The firelight caused the air to shimmer. As I looked at Amos, the rough clothes that draped his tall, strong frame faded and changed into a loincloth, moccasins, beads. He hefted a war shield on one arm. The fingers of his other hand closed around a spear.

Caught up in the vision, I cried, "Amos, come with us! We

are going to head for the mountains to the west where we will set up our own village—"

"I will stay here near the big ships. Someday I will hide on board. I will go home." He said it with finality, a fact already accomplished. "Now eat." He rose and ladled soup into a bowl. After handing the bowl to me, along with a spoon, he said, "Berkeley's soldiers are afraid. Some have deserted. Berkeley has built a mud and log wall—"

"I saw it."

"He has placed cannons along the wall."

I nodded. "That will be a problem, but I won't be around to watch Bacon solve it. As soon as I get those chains off Naokan and Pomanah—"

"Two Susquehannock brothers?"

"One brother. Naokan. Pomanah is his sister."

"A woman for your village," he said solemnly.

I felt my face grow hot when I realized what he was implying. "She's a healer. She makes medicine from roots and leaves."

"A woman who is a healer. That is even better. One of my women was a healer."

I caught a slight smile in his voice, which reminded me of my father in a teasing mood.

Stung, I muttered, "You don't understand." I quickly finished the soup and placed the bowl on the hearth. "Look, I need to leave—"

"Swimming upriver will be hard when you're carrying a hammer and chisel."

I'd already thought of that. "I plan to tie them to a log and push them ahead of me."

He shook his head. "What will the soldiers think when they see a log floating upriver against the current?"

"I'll have to take my chances—"

"No," he interrupted. "Miss Charlotte has a boat. I will get my fishing pole, row you past the barricade and set you down near the woods."

"But the sentries—"

"— know I fish at night," he interrupted. "They see only an ignorant slave and pay no heed to what I do. Some night when it is dark and stormy, I will board a ship that is headed for home and hide in the hold. Later, when people find the mistress's boat drifting empty toward the sea, they will think I fell into the river and drowned."

"But how will you know which ship to board?"

"The stink. A slave ship stinks of rotting flesh."

My father's words returned to me: *It is better to die in freedom than live in bondage.*

Worry spurred me to my feet. I had to get back to Bacon's camp. I had to set Naokan and Pomanah free.

"Where are the tools?"

"Here." Amos rose and drew them forth from under his cot, along with a canvas bag that had a long leather strap. "But first we must change the way you look."

He rejoined me at the hearth where he rubbed soot over my face and hands until my skin was almost as dark as his. Then he gave me a cap to hide my hair and a long gray shirt, heavily patched, to cover my wet clothes. I tucked my moccasins into my belt beneath the shirt and blackened my bare feet.

"If we meet someone, hang your head and shuffle your feet," he told me. "I learned this from the lion. The lion is strong, the lion is brave. But when the lion hunts the ibex, he first crawls through the grass on his belly to hide his lion heart."

One with the snake, one with the wind.

"Did you hunt with the lion, Amos?"

"I hunted the lion himself."

He slid the hammer and chisel into the canvas bag and

hefted the strap onto my shoulder. My body sagged to one side, pulled down by the weight of the tools. Already my mind scurried ahead, wondering how I could get Naokan and Pomanah away from their guards and how I could strike the irons from their ankles without attracting attention.

Freedom. It had become a living thing for me, a person shouting from a hilltop, "Hurry, hurry!"

Amos handed me a fishing pole and got another for himself. Only a few specks of candlelight showed through the pierced tin shutters of the lantern that Amos carried, but it was enough to cast a dim glow over the path as we made our way to the river.

"Halt. Who goes there?" demanded a sentry.

Amos stepped forward and lifted the lantern, so that the flecks of light danced like fireflies across his face.

"Miss Charlotte's Amos."

I saw the outline of the sentry's body, which at first had been stiff and straight, now relax. "Amos. I've told you before, you should fish at sunset, not after dark."

"Yes, Sir. Have to do my chores first, Sir."

"Who is that with you, Amos?"

"Beelzebub. Belongs to a governor's man, Sir."

Amos swung the lantern my way. Although my muscles tensed, I forced myself to stand still, shoulders drooping, head sagging.

The sentry snorted with laughter. "Beelzebub? Named for the devil himself, and well he looks it! All right, go along. If you catch any fish, bring some to me."

"Yes, Sir."

Amos led me to a pier where several rowboats were tied. A slight wind had come up, creating waves that slapped gently against the pilings. Amos tapped me on the shoulder and motioned toward one of the boats. I scrambled from the pier down into the boat, juggling my pole and the bag. Amos handed me the lantern and his own pole before casting off the line and climbing down to join me. He settled the oars into the locks and rowed with swift, strong strokes out into the river, past a ghostly line of sloops that sighed in the night like restless sleepers.

"Blow out the candle," he whispered.

When I did so, the night closed around us like a suffocating blanket. Within seconds, however, the darkness thinned, revealing a river that gleamed with star glow.

"What if—" I began.

"Shuuuu."

Bend, pull, bend, pull, Amos dragged at the oars in a steady rhythm. The town slid past, and then the barricade, lit by scattered bonfires. Amos continued rowing for almost a mile before putting into shore.

"What happens when you go back without me?" I asked.

"I'll tell the sentry you got sick and I put you ashore at a different place."

"Will he believe you?"

He chuckled softly. "He will if I take him some fish."

"Then I wish you a good catch. Good-bye, Amos. When I think of you I'll think of lions."

"May your mountains to the west be filled with meat," he said.

I climbed from the boat and he pushed off at once, soon drifting out of sight. I tugged on my moccasins, repositioned the bag over my shoulder, and slipped into the darkness of the forest.

Fourteen

TRACKING A PATH through the wilderness at night, where landmarks are no longer visible, is a difficult task. Although I tried to steer by the north star, I became lost and had to hole up until daybreak. I was awakened just before dawn by birds caroling their morning songs.

I climbed a tall tree and squinted toward the horizon, where clouds floated like pale ships in a pink sea. A distant hill, broken on one side as if sliced by a dull knife, gave me my bearings at last. I climbed down and set off at a trot, reaching Bacon's camp in time for breakfast.

Before entering the camp, however, I hid the bag with the tools in a dark cavity under a tree root. Then I backtracked and approached the camp from a different direction.

"Hallooo, it's Robert," I called to warn the sentry of my arrival.

When I drew near I saw that the sentry was Drummond, wearing his usual tartan baldric and broad-brimmed hat with jaunty plaid cockade.

"So, lad, you're back." He grinned as he looked me up and down. "With those clothes and that black on your skin, you look like a runaway slave, come to join our army."

"Where is the general?"

"Near the cook fire, the last time I saw him. That way."

He pointed and I set off through the camp, dodging soldiers with uncombed hair and disheveled clothes. Several lay on the ground, shivering and groaning beneath their blankets, and I knew they had been struck down by the fever, which claimed more victims every day.

I found Bacon slumped on a log near the fire. His eyes, always deep set, looked more sunken and shadowed than ever, as if he had not slept.

"General Bacon?"

He roused with a start. "Robert. What did you learn?"

Quickly I made my report, leaving out any mention of Amos as I described the barricade, the pending arrival of troops from England, the departure of the women from Jamestown.

Bacon's brows drew together while he pondered what I had said. "A barricade," he muttered. "They'll blow us to pieces before we can—" He paused, thinking hard. Then he straightened. "You say some of the women have been sent to Greenspring for safety?"

"Yes."

Suddenly his mouth quirked and widened into a grin. "Berkeley, always the Cavalier. Robert, I think you've just told me how we can take Jamestown. With the king's troops on their way—I suspected that, of course. We must act quickly."

With that he rose and strode away.

A soldier and a camp woman stirred pots of stew beside the fire.

The woman, looking tired but cheerful, called, "Here, boy, would you like something to eat?"

When I nodded she ladled a steamy mixture of corn mush and meat into a pan. My stomach growled in response. Grabbing up a spoon, I gulped the food, blowing on each bite to keep it from burning my tongue. After licking the last of the mush from the spoon, I dropped the pan into a barrel filled with greasy water.

She grinned. "Maybe I should douse you in that barrel, too. You could do with a bath."

"Not now. Where are the Susquehannock prisoners, do you know?"

The soldier turned an angry scowl in my direction. "They

could be dead for all I care. Those savages killed my neighbors last spring."

I took a step back from the murder in his eyes. What if I were too late? What if someone like this man had already taken revenge on Naokan and Pomanah?

I ran through the camp, seeking first one way and then another, like a weather vane driven by a fickle wind. The sound of derisive laughter drew my attention toward several men clustered in a clearing. They had sticks in their hands and were poking at something in the center of their circle. Twice I had seen soldiers corner an animal, once a possum, once a bear cub, and torment it to death for sport. These men, dirty, dressed in rags, did not look like Bacon's regular troops. They were, I decided, some of the indentureds who had run away from their masters to join with Bacon. Although my father had been innocent of the crime for which he had been transported, he had told me about other indentureds who were indeed ruffians and rakehells, criminals of the worst order.

I veered in their direction, drawn by some premonition that they had cornered something other than a bear. Sure enough, Naokan crouched in the center of the circle, fists clenched, eyes so fierce as he surveyed his tormentors that no one could mistake him any longer for being blind. A tall man with a red beard and crooked teeth stood to one side, hands clenched around Pomanah's arms. He laughed when she struggled to get free as one of the men jabbed his stick into Naokan's chest. Naokan staggered backward, encumbered by the shackles, and almost fell before managing, with difficulty, to regain his balance.

Fire filled my brain.

"Aiieee!"

Screaming the Susquehannock war cry, I charged the man who had just jabbed Naokan. He started to turn toward me but before he could take action, I jumped on his back and rode him to the ground. As I rolled off, I grabbed the stick from his hands. When he rose to his knees, I clouted him over the head.

I turned and swung the stick hard against the side of another man's neck. He went down as if he'd been shot. I snatched up his club and darted forward to take my place beside Naokan.

"Here," I said, tossing him the club.

We circled, back to back, eyeing the men who surrounded us. Surprise filled their faces, followed by rage.

"Another damned Susquee!" one of them yelled and charged forward.

Naokan felled the man with a blow across the knees. The other men howled and descended upon us, sticks whistling in the air. One stick cracked down across my shoulder, another struck me in the middle of the back, forcing air from my lungs.

Blam.

Gunfire exploded over our heads.

"Stop!" shouted a voice that crackled with authority. "Stop or I will shoot you."

Our attackers faltered and fell back. I straightened, breathing hard while wincing against the pain in my shoulder. I turned toward Naokan, and we shared a look that removed any barriers that might have remained between us.

"Robert, what is the meaning of this?"

Bacon stood before us, pistol clenched in one hand, his face suffused with anger.

"This is Naokan," I said. "My brother."

Fifteen

BACON LOOKED BACK and forth between Naokan and me, his face a study of surprise, doubt, anger. He lifted one hand and pointed a finger at Naokan.

"He is a murderer. He killed your family."

"Naokan tried to stop the war chief," I interrupted. "He—"

"You lied to me. You said you hated Susquehannocks." The accusation in Bacon's voice pierced me like a sword. "Is he blind or not?"

He stepped forward, peering into Naokan's eyes. Naokan stared back, his chin high, his face impassive.

"You don't have to tell me, it's obvious he can see." Bacon turned to me. "Now I know why you wanted their shackles removed. You planned to help them escape."

"I—"

Bacon grabbed my shoulders and jerked me away from Naokan. "You're a Virginian and a Christian. Indians are spawn of the Devil himself."

"But—"

"General!" Drummond strode into the clearing, followed by Hansford. "We've dispatched the advance troops as you ordered. The other troops are ready for your command."

Bacon dug his fingers into my shoulders and shook me once, hard. "I don't have time to deal with you now." He thrust me toward Hansford. "Take his weapons away and don't let him out of your sight." To the ruffians who had been tormenting Naokan he said, "Report to your commanding officers. Drummond, guard these two Indians during the march. See that they don't escape. I want them alive when we capture Berkeley."

"Yes, Sir."

Bacon stalked away, shouting orders to everyone in sight, while Hansford grabbed my arm and pulled me to one side where we could not be overheard.

"You have a penchant for trouble, Robert. What have you done now?"

I told him the whole story.

"Naokan's uncle hated white people and would have killed all of us if he could," I finished. "But Naokan and Pomanah—"

"Do you really trust them, Robert?" Hansford eyed me seriously. "Are you sure Bacon isn't right, that they'd cut your throat, given the chance?"

"They would not."

He continued as if I hadn't spoken. "God knows they would feel justified, since we did destroy their village. Of course, they destroyed your plantation—"

"Not Naokan, not Pomanah. They were not a part of that. Hansford, I need your help."

"To do what?"

"There is a place outside camp where I hid a bag. I have to go get it."

"What is in that bag?"

"Don't ask. Just let me go."

Hansford shook his head. "I'm not supposed to let you out of my sight. In fact, I'm supposed to take your weapons."

"I don't have my pistol with me. It's wrapped in my blanket, along with my boots and tinderbox, back near your campsite. I do have my knife, but I need it, and I need that bag, and I'm going to get it. The only way you can stop me is to shoot me."

"You know I won't do that."

As we confronted each other, I noticed for the first time that his face had aged over the summer, as if an artist had drawn thin lines above his brows and down his cheeks on either side of his nose and mouth.

"Robert, what would your father say about all this?" he asked.

My stomach twisted in a painful knot. "My father always told me to do what is right. But now—" I paused, groping for words. "Bacon is wrong when he says all Indians are bad. And Okahanah—he was wrong when he said the same thing about white people. And the king. He's wrong when he brands a starving mother for stealing food for her child. And Berkeley—" I paused, burdened by the grief they had caused. "All I know is that I must get Naokan and Pomanah away from here. If I can help them reach those mountains beyond Virginia . . ."

Hansford's eyes had searched my face intently while I spoke. As my words trailed off, he said, "Even if they get away, you don't have to go with them."

"What do you mean?"

"Your father was a decent, hard-working man. I admired him, and I have come to admire you, too—your courage, your spunk. I have sons, too, and I hope they grow up to be like you. You could live with us."

The offer came as such a surprise that for one moment I could not speak.

"You don't have to answer now," Hansford said, seeming to sense my confusion.

"I—this is . . . thank you. I feel honored that you would ask. But—"

He waited.

"Hansford, I can't stay. Naokan is my brother, Pomanah is my sister. They need me."

"But once they've escaped, they will return to their own people, and then you—"

"They can't return. When Naokan defied Okahanah, he lost all rights as a Susquehannock warrior. No village will take him in. When winter comes—look, we have to head for the mountains now, find a safe place, lay in a supply of food, build a lodge before the snows fall."

Hansford straightened his shoulders and nodded, his face grim. "Who knows, you may be safer there than here. This blasted war . . . All right, come along. We'll collect our gear and then we'll look for that bag you need."

He led the way and I followed, dodging through the turmoil of a camp that was preparing to march.

Sixteen

EVEN THOUGH I had noted landmarks when hiding the bag, I now had difficulty relocating the tree. While I was searching, the troops surged past, led by Bacon on a tall horse. Boots and hooves thudded against the earth like fists beating a giant drum. Somewhere in that crowd Naokan and Pomanah were being swept along toward the coming battle.

"There!" I cried, spotting the tree at last. I ran forward and then stopped abruptly when I realized my mistake. "Wrong one."

"What are you looking for?" Hansford asked.

"A pine tree. Partially uprooted. Leaning against another pine."

"I'll go this way, you go that way," Hansford said.

The sound of the army had long since died away by the time Hansford shouted, off to my left, "Is this it?"

I hurried to join him and sighed with relief when I saw that he had indeed found the spot.

"Yes, that's it."

I knelt and dug the bag out from under the roots. When I rose and hoisted the bag over one shoulder, the hammer and chisel, jostling against each other, clanked like iron bells.

"You told me not to ask what's in there, but I can guess," Hansford said.

"You'd probably be right. Let's go."

I strode forward, following the army's path: churned earth, broken bushes. In order to reduce the amount I would have to carry, I had discarded my coat, blanket, and boots back in camp, preferring to wear moccasins with my breeches. I had also kept Amos's shirt because it hung almost to my knees and covered the knife, pistol, powder horn, and pouch of pistol balls, which

Hansford had allowed me to keep. He had also allowed me to bring my tinderbox, which now rode deep inside my breeches' pocket.

We had traveled about a mile when we came upon a soldier and the woman who had fed me breakfast. They were huddled beside the prone, shivering body of another soldier whose sunken eyes and gray skin told me that the illness had progressed beyond recovery. Hansford knelt beside him.

"Spencer?"

"Ye—yes, Sir," the sick man gasped between chattering teeth.

"When—?" Hansford began.

"Yesterday," the woman replied. "He came down with it yesterday."

"Tell Bacon I—I'll come just as soon . . . when I'm feeling better," the sick man said, clutching Hansford's hand.

Hansford extended his other hand to touch the man's forehead in a gesture so tender that it tugged at my heart, bringing to mind my mother's touch when I had struggled through pneumonia.

"I will tell him. You stay here and rest." He gently smoothed the man's tousled hair while glancing toward the others. "Thank you, Margaret. Thank you, Sergeant. Please stay here with him until—" He broke off the words and I realized he had almost said, "Until it's over."

"I will do that, Captain," the soldier said. "Good luck in Jamestown."

"We will need that luck," Hansford replied.

He rose and we took our leave, once more following the army's trail. When we were beyond the sick man's hearing, Hansford said, "Poor Spencer. More people have died from the fever this year than from all our arrows or guns."

I gave him a level look. "That's why I wear this salve."

He snorted with sudden laughter and clapped me on the shoulder. "I can tell you right now, Robert, my offer to let you live with us did not include that smell."

We caught up with the army near Greenspring. I noticed with surprise that many of the men carried shovels as well as muskets. As we advanced through the ranks, searching for Naokan and Pomanah, we heard a commotion up ahead that included the shrieks and cries of many women, sounding more angry than in pain.

"What's going on?" Hansford muttered.

He strode forward and I pushed after him, drawn by curiosity. Visible over the shoulders of the soldiers sat Bacon on his horse, looking down at something I could not see. Whatever it was, the protests came from there so I edged closer. As the scene shifted with the movement of the soldiers, I saw one woman, two women, many women, dressed in fine gowns and obviously highborn. Their voices mingled together in a cacophony of outrage.

"I demand that you take us home at once!"

"What do you think you are doing?"

"The governor shall hear of this!"

"Ladies, ladies, calm yourselves," called Bacon in ringing tones that cut through the bedlam. "You will not be harmed, I assure you."

"Sir, you are not a gentleman," called one of the women in disdainful tones.

Bacon laughed in a display of mischief and merriment unlike his usual serious demeanor. "It was our own great bard who said, 'All's fair in love and war.' Ladies, you are going to help me take Jamestown."

"Never!"

The woman who snapped that word stood only a few feet away from me. She flounced around, turning her back on Bacon, her chin held high, her lips pressed together in a thin white line. As her eyes raked the crowd, I saw her expression change from anger to startled surprise. She swung her gaze back to lock with mine.

"Aunt Charlotte," I said.

Seventeen

THE MEN AROUND me edged apart, leaving me face-to-face with my aunt.

"I should have known you'd be a part of this outrage," she said.

"What's going on? What are you doing here?" I asked.

"We have been abducted against our will." Her eyes burned with a fierce anger that rivaled the blazing midday sun.

Apart from a few curious glances from those closest to us, we were ignored. Most eyes seemed to be focused on Bacon and the larger scene. I glanced toward him as he waved one arm expansively and announced, "Ladies, a nice walk together on a pleasant September day. A little stroll to Jamestown to pay our compliments to the governor."

Renewed outcries from the captured women greeted his words.

"No!"

"Inexcusable!"

"Let us go at once!"

I turned back to my aunt. "Are you all right? Are you hurt?"

"I am not all right. My wrist is bruised and my ankle is twisted."

Another woman appeared beside her, a work-worn woman dressed in homespun.

"Joanna!" I cried.

"They came to Greenspring an hour ago, the soldiers," she said. "Overpowered the men Berkeley had sent to protect us. Tied them up and left them in the stables. Came to the kitchens and stole all our aprons. Robbed the linen closets. Took all the tablecloths. The bedsheets."

Bacon's advance troops.

"But why?" I asked.

She shook her head in obvious bewilderment.

"Ladies, aprons. White aprons to protect your fine gowns," Bacon announced. He gestured toward several soldiers who stepped forward, their arms piled high with linens. "Put these on, please. We have ladies-in-waiting to assist you."

Sarah Drummond stepped into the circle, followed by a number of other camp women whose carelessly laced bodices and short skirts proclaimed their free attitude toward life.

They each took a handful of linens from the soldiers and advanced toward the prisoners, who shrank away at their approach.

All amusement vanished from Bacon's face.

"You *will* put on these aprons," he commanded in the cold, hard voice of authority.

"Cousin, I demand to know why you are doing this."

A middle-aged woman of aristocratic bearing stepped toward the center of the circle, her angular nose jutting toward Bacon in proud defiance.

Hansford appeared beside me.

"Who is that?" I asked, gesturing toward the woman.

"The elder Mr. Bacon's wife," he muttered.

Surprise splashed through me. "Bacon's cousin? The man who helped him back in June?"

"Yes." Then he murmured as if to himself, "Oh, Nathaniel." His voice carried a note of despair.

Holding out a couple of aprons, Sarah Drummond approached my aunt and Joanna.

"Good day, Miss Bromworth," she said.

My aunt's face twisted with contempt. "You, Sarah Drummond. You and your husband, who once sat at the governor's table and toasted the king. Now you drink with rebels and strumpets."

"And good company it is," replied Sarah. "Put this on."

"I will not!"

Sarah shrugged. "Then risk getting shot."

"Sh—shot?" my aunt stammered. "What are you talking about?"

Ignoring her, Sarah handed the aprons to Joanna. "See if you can persuade her. You must wear one, too. I certainly intend to wear mine."

She turned and stalked away.

I saw that the other captured women, despite continued protests, were donning the aprons.

"Do you know what this is about?" Joanna asked me.

"No."

Drummond appeared, escorting Naokan and Pomanah, whose chained ankles clanked as they shuffled through the dust. One of the camp women joined them and jerked the feathers from Pomanah's hair before tying a long white apron around her neck and waist. Dismay tingled through me as though I'd been brushed by lightning. Naokan shot me a look that asked the same question Joanna had just asked. I shook my head.

"Are we ready? Good," Bacon said. "Ladies, you will spread out in a line at the front of the march, a white shield to protect my men."

"But this is villainous!" my aunt gasped.

Mrs. Bacon pointed an accusing finger at Bacon. "Hiding behind women's aprons is the act of a coward, Nathaniel."

"Once we get our position established and our defenses in place, you'll be released," he replied. "All right, ladies, line up."

Bacon's women put on their own white aprons and prodded the captured women, including Pomanah, into a lengthy horizontal line in front of the army.

"Please, Mistress, you must wear this," Joanna murmured, holding out the apron.

Angry purple splotches bloomed in Aunt Charlotte's cheeks, matching the color of her dress. Nevertheless, she took the apron and put it on. Joanna donned her own apron and then gently pulled my aunt forward into the line. Thus it was that they ended up next to Pomanah.

Meanwhile, Bacon rode back and forth on his horse shouting additional instructions to his men, who now fell into formation behind the women.

"In all my years in the king's service I never marched into battle behind a woman, never!" one of them grumbled.

His companion laughed, a harsh snort. "You know Berkeley won't shoot women. At least this gives us a chance to get close to Berkeley's troops before the firing starts."

Bacon drew his sword and pointed toward Jamestown in a commanding gesture. As his horse moved forward, the line of women followed, urged into action by Sarah Drummond, who marched up and down shouting commands as if she were an officer. Naokan shuffled along as fast as he could behind Pomanah. I fell into step beside him.

"We are not going to escape," he stated flatly.

"Don't give up yet."

But what could I do to create a diversion? Shoot Bacon or Drummond? That wouldn't work. The soldiers would be on top of us in a second. If I waited until the battle actually started, could I pull Naokan and Pomanah away from the soldiers and into the trees? That seemed unlikely.

My head pounded with plans, echoing the sound of the boots that thudded around us. As we proceeded over the rough ground, my aunt's limp grew worse. Finally, with a cry, she fell to one knee. I darted forward and took her arm.

"Here, Aunt Charlotte, let me help you."

"I don't need help."

But when she tried to rise, her ankle gave way and she fell again. I draped one of her arms over my shoulder and tried to lift her up, but the weight of her body, added to the weight of the tools that hung from my other shoulder, proved more than I could manage. Hansford pushed into the line and took my aunt's other arm. Between the two of us we got her to her feet. By then the relentless crush of the army was bearing down upon us. We staggered forward, dragging my aunt between us. At last she regained her balance and hobbled along as best she could, favoring her injured ankle.

I felt a tap on my arm and glanced toward Pomanah.

"I can help," she said.

She withdrew her medicine pouch from under the apron and handed me a sprig of dried weed. "Tell her to chew this for the pain."

I took the weed and extended it toward my aunt. "She says this herb will help you."

My aunt looked askance toward Pomanah. "She is a savage. And she is filthy."

"She is a healer."

"Robert is right, Miss Bromworth," Hansford put in. "I've seen this girl do amazing things with roots and leaves."

To my surprise, my aunt paused long enough to take the sprig and place it in her mouth. I knew then that her pain must be severe. She chewed and swallowed before making a face.

"Faugh! I hope I have not been poisoned."

Joanna peered with open curiosity toward Pomanah before turning to me. "You understood what she said?"

"Yes. She's been my friend for a long time."

Still grimacing, my aunt exclaimed, "Your mother would be appalled if she knew that."

"My mother was friends with Pomanah, too."

Unbidden, the image of my mother's arrow-pierced body rose before me. And yet I was sure my mother would want me to save Pomanah and Naokan if I could. Anger, grief, hatred, loyalty, love . . . they ran through me like water from different streams pouring into a river to become inextricably mixed. It was too much to think about at that moment. I shifted the bag with the tools to the center of my back, trying to redistribute the weight so that I could provide a firmer support for my aunt as we marched in Bacon's strange parade toward the war with Berkeley.

Eighteen

WE REACHED THE peninsula an hour after leaving Greenspring. Protected in front by our white-aproned shield, we crossed the isthmus toward Jamestown. The men whom Berkeley had posted there as guards fled to the safety of the barricade when they saw us coming.

"Look at 'em run!" cried a soldier just behind me.

Laughter and shouts of triumph rose from the other men, but Aunt Charlotte, still supported by Hansford and me, let out a sobbing wail. When we were within striking distance of the barricade, Bacon called a halt.

"Dig!" he shouted. "Throw up a breastwork!"

Sarah Drummond pulled my aunt forward into the line of women that protected us from Berkeley's guns, while Joanna hurried to support her. The soldiers with shovels set to work, gouging a trench in the marshy soil and piling the dirt in front to form a rampart. Hansford and I found stout sticks and dug, too, using our bare hands to toss the loosened earth onto the growing mound in front of the trench.

Finally I straightened and wiped the sleeve of my shirt across my perspiring forehead. Hansford straightened, too, while glancing toward the women.

"Some people are going to condemn Nathaniel for using women in this way," he said, "but I'll have to admit, it's working."

His voice carried a note of reluctant admiration.

"And when we get this finished, what then?" I asked.

"Then we take up defensive positions while the women move out of the line of fire."

I glanced around to make sure no one else was listening before murmuring, "Hansford, I need your help again."

"You want me to help your friends escape."

"You know what will happen if I don't get them away from here."

"Some of our own soldiers—"

"That's right," I interrupted. "Some of our own soldiers may shoot them if Berkeley's men don't do it first."

"They hate the Susquehannocks. Robert, I do, too. The horror I've seen—"

"Are we any better? That day at Naokan's village . . ." I paused, sickened by the images that filled my head. "Hansford, these men shot Susquehannock children who tried to run."

Hansford's face hardened into granite. "Just as the Susquehannocks shot your brother and sister when they tried to run."

The memory pained my chest with a thrust as sharp as a knife. "It has to stop. On both sides. It has to stop. All I ask is that you distract Drummond long enough for me to get Naokan and Pomanah into the woods near the river. When the women leave . . . that might be a good time. There will be a lot of confusion then."

He pulled his gaze away from mine and stared into space for a long moment. "All right, I'll see what I can do."

He bent once more to his task, and so did I. Shovels up and down the line thudded into the earth in a steady rhythm. Sand and pebbles, flung out onto the rising mound of dirt, splattered like hail.

"Mistress!" wailed a voice. Joanna's voice.

"Something's happened to my aunt," I exclaimed to Hansford.

I dropped my shovel, jumped from the trench, and scrambled over the mound to find Joanna kneeling beside my aunt's crumpled body.

"She's fainted," Joanna said. "The strain—"

"Take her legs. Let's move her into the trench."

I grasped my aunt's shoulders while Joanna grabbed her ankles. Together, we struggled up the mound and down the other side. Hansford helped us lower my aunt into the trench where we laid her on the dirt. Joanna knelt and loosened the buttons of my aunt's bodice down to an immodest level, a fact that would have caused my aunt distress had she known.

"Water," Joanna muttered.

She accepted a canteen from Hansford and sprinkled some of its contents over my aunt's face and neck.

"We must move her to a cooler place," Joanna said.

An idea took shape in my mind. I scrambled out of the trench and over the mound once more to the line of women.

"Close the ranks," Sarah Drummond was shouting as she pointed toward the space left by Joanna's and my aunt's departure. "Fill that gap."

As the women began to shuffle around, I grabbed Pomanah's arm, pulling her out of line. The woman next to her glanced in my direction, and I recognized the long nose and haughty brow of Bacon's cousin's wife.

"Mistress Bromworth . . . she is taken ill," I explained. "We need this Indian girl's medicine."

Without waiting for a reply, I dragged Pomanah up the mound and over the edge of the trench. The shackles around her ankles rang as she tumbled down beside my aunt.

"What are you doing?" Hansford demanded.

I grabbed my bag of tools, which lay nearby.

"This is our chance. You and Joanna, you carry my aunt down the trench toward those woods." I gestured in the direction of the river. "Pomanah and I will follow. You're an officer. No one will ask questions if you seem to be in charge of a medical emergency."

"What about your other friend?"

"Right now let's get Pomanah to safety."

Joanna grabbed Hansford's sleeve with one hand while motioning toward my aunt with the other. "We must hurry. I've seen people die from heat sickness."

"All right."

He and Joanna lifted my aunt's limp body and struggled down the length of the trench while Pomanah and I followed close behind. I kept a frown on my face and a firm grip on Pomanah's arm, as if I had her in custody.

"Make way, make way," Hansford commanded over and over while we edged through the long line of perspiring soldiers who continued to dig and fling dirt with barely a glance in our direction.

When we reached the end of the trench, we saw that we would have to traverse at least twenty feet of open space to reach the protection of the trees.

Hansford glanced toward me with a question on his face, but I already had a plan.

"I'll help carry her now," I said, taking over from Joanna. "Joanna, you walk right beside Hansford so that your apron is visible to Berkeley's men." Switching to Susquehannock, I said, "Pomanah, you walk next to me."

The three soldiers at that end of the trench stopped digging to lean on their shovels.

"What's going on, Captain?"

"She has heat sickness," Hansford told them. "Bacon has pledged that no harm shall come to any of these women. We are taking her to the shade of those trees." In a firm voice he added, "Carry on, men. We must get this barricade finished as soon as possible so that the rest of the women can leave."

"Yes, Sir."

My heart sped up to double time as we climbed from the trench. I was certain that none of Berkeley's men would shoot us under the circumstances, but I was not so sure that someone from our side would not try to stop us. If Bacon saw what was happening, would he come to investigate? What about Sarah Drummond?

We must have crossed that open space in less than a minute, but it seemed like an hour. By the time we reached the trees I was drenched in sweat. We carried my aunt deeper into the trees and laid her on a grassy sward near a small stream. Joanna dipped the corner of her apron into the stream and began bathing my aunt's face. Pomanah knelt beside Joanna and lifted my aunt's petticoats to remove her shoe and examine her swollen ankle. With relief I slipped the heavy bag from my shoulder and stepped to one side to join Hansford.

"I must get back," he said.

"I know. Hansford, thank you. For this." I paused and finished lamely, "For everything."

"Good luck, Robert."

"You, too, Sir."

We shook hands and he turned to go, but I called out, "Wait! Put on Pomanah's apron. And take off your hat and stuff it inside your shirt to give yourself a bosom."

A grin spread across his face. "That's a good idea, I'll have to admit."

While he donned the apron I asked Joanna for her white neck scarf to tie around his hair. When the masquerade was complete, I looked him over with a critical eye.

"There. That should confuse Berkeley's soldiers long enough for you to make it safely back to the trench. If you have a chance to do so without attracting attention, please tell Naokan what has happened. Yes, he understands English."

Hansford shook his head in mock reproval. "All that time you let us think . . . you are a rascal, you know that?"

As he strode away, I hurried to kneel beside Joanna and Pomanah. My aunt began to moan as a chill shook her body, and I saw that her skin had turned the color of dirty wool.

"It's not heat sickness," Joanna said. "She has the fever."

Nineteen

ALARMED BY JOANNA'S pronouncement, I touched my aunt's clammy forehead. She opened her eyes and stared blankly up at me as if I were not there. Then her eyes moved to a spot beyond my left shoulder and joy dawned on her face, transforming her from an aging woman into a girl.

"Anne," she whispered.

My heart jumped with shock at the sound of my mother's name. Although I knew my aunt had to be wandering in her mind, I still glanced over my shoulder, half expecting to see my mother standing there.

"Anne, you've come . . ."

My aunt's voice trailed away and I turned back as she once more closed her eyes. Her hand, which she had extended in the direction of her vision, fell limply to her side.

My breath caught in my throat. Was she dead? No, a pulse throbbed faintly in her neck. I rocked back on my heels and looked up to find both Joanna and Pomanah regarding me with steady eyes. Muffled commands bounced toward us through the trees, as if Bacon were shouting orders. The thud of shovels stopped. More commands. Scattered cries of women.

"We must move deeper into the woods," I said. "If the soldiers decide to circle around through here—"

Joanna nodded before I could finish. Again she and I lifted my aunt's limp body and struggled through the trees in the direction of the river. Pomanah shuffled along beside us, bending occasionally to disentangle twigs and leaves from the chain that connected her ankles. When we came to a boulder that brooded like a mother hen over a clutch of stones, I said, "Stop for a minute."

After we had laid my aunt on a bed of matted leaves, I slipped the bag from my shoulders and pulled out the hammer and chisel.

"Pomanah, let's get rid of those shackles."

She came forward while I selected a large flat stone to use for an anvil. Joanna ripped a piece from the bottom of her petticoat and wrapped it around Pomanah's right foot and ankle, offering some protection should the chisel slip. I positioned the chisel over the lock and lifted the hammer.

"Ready?"

Pomanah nodded.

Praying that I wouldn't accidentally break her bones instead of the iron, I brought the hammer down. The clang of metal against metal rang through the trees like the knell of a church bell.

"They'll hear that," Joanna said.

More shouts from the meadow joined with increased cries from the women, as shrill as a flight of birds. I heard the thud of running feet, shrieks, a shot.

"Not over that noise," I said. "Besides, these have to come off."

I lifted the hammer and struck again. And again. On the fifth stroke the lock broke and the bracelet fell from Pomanah's ankle, exposing flesh as raw as a strip of butchered meat.

"God have mercy," Joanna whispered.

Pomanah didn't flinch. "The other one," she said.

That time I managed to break the lock with only four strokes. While Pomanah took salve from her medicine pouch and bent to doctor her ankles, I gathered up the broken shackles and placed them in the bag, along with the hammer and chisel.

Joanna frowned. "Why are you keeping those?"

"They're good iron," I said. "We can use them to make tools when we head west into the mountains."

"You're going with them." She nodded toward Pomanah.

"Yes."

"What do you expect to find there?"

"Freedom."

"Freedom." She breathed the word as if it were a prayer.

"You can come with us if you want," I said.

For a moment her face twisted with longing. "I can't leave her, not when she's so sick."

"No. But if she dies—"

"Some live through the fever. I must save her if I can."

"Why, Joanna? I thought you didn't like her."

"She a cold woman, but she isn't mean, not like some, not like Josiah Wheeler and others I've heard of. She works me hard, but she treats me fairly, and Amos, too. I will not leave her during these troubles."

Less that twenty-four hours ago Amos and I had landed near this spot. I wondered if he had made it safely home the night before and if he had now been commandeered by Berkeley to join the soldiers on the wall. Would he ever find his way back to the lions? And what would happen to Joanna three years from now when her servitude ended? Where would she go? What could she do?

"Joanna, before I go away . . ." I paused, considering my idea, and decided it was good. "I want to give you my land. For when you are free. I'd like for Amos to live there, too, if Bacon wins and frees the slaves."

"But—"

I spoke quickly, interrupting her. "If Berkeley wins, I have no land. It's forfeit to the crown. But if Bacon wins—"

"What if you decide to come back someday?" she asked.

"Then I'll expect you to take me in; but I won't be back, I already know that."

Pomanah rose and stood with her head cocked.

"Someone's coming," she said.

"Hide," I commanded, pointing toward a nearby thicket.

Without argument Pomanah and Joanna slipped away and disappeared into the shadows. I grabbed the hammer from the bag and turned in the direction Pomanah had indicated, placing myself between my aunt and the unknown intruder. Soon I heard the snapping of twigs, the scuffling of stones and dirt.

"Robert?"

The voice sounded like Hansford's, but I couldn't be sure. Still clutching the hammer, I moved forward. My heart bounded with relief when Hansford appeared through the trees, followed by Naokan. Dropping the hammer, I rushed forward to clasp Naokan's arm in the Susquehannock greeting.

"How did you—" I began.

"Bacon ordered the women away and they fled like frightened geese," Hansford said. "I shoved your friend toward the running women, told him to head for the woods and to fall when I fired my pistol. He did, and I yelled that I'd killed him. Then I dodged through the line of women and dragged him into the trees."

"Hansford—"

"No time. You must get away from here. Now."

He glanced toward Joanna and Pomanah, who had left their hiding place to join us. As Joanna knelt beside my aunt, Hansford turned back to me with a question in his eyes.

"She has the fever," I explained. "I need to take her where she can be cared for."

"Try to find a boat and cross the river. Maybe you can take her to a plantation on the other side."

More shouts echoed from the direction of the meadow.

"I must go," Hansford said. "Godspeed, Robert."

He hurried away without looking back. Pomanah pointed toward Naokan's shackles.

"Free my brother."

I led the way to the anvil rock. Again Joanna used the petticoat strips to shield fragile flesh while I struck the iron from Naokan's legs. As Pomanah bent over Naokan to spread salve on the oozing bands of abraded skin that circled his ankles, I felt anger spark within me and flame into rage. Had Bacon appeared in the clearing at that moment, I would have knocked his brains out with the hammer.

The popping of musket fire fell through the trees like hail to be answered by the loud *whump* of cannon.

"It's begun," Joanna said. "Can we find a boat?"

The only boats I knew of were in Jamestown. To go there now, in daylight, with the battle engaged, would be suicide, and I was not willing to risk dying at this point when freedom was so close at hand.

"Stay here," I told the women. "Naokan and I will scout and see what we can find."

Naokan rose, shaking first one foot and then the other as if to free himself from the ghost of the shackles.

"One with the wind, my brother," I said.

"One with the snake," he answered.

Slipping in silence through the trees, we headed together for the river.

Twenty

WHEN WE REACHED the edge of the woods beside the river, Naokan touched my arm and pointed toward a small dock, crudely built, to which an old rowboat was tied. I had been prepared for a difficult task, but here lay the answer to our needs, set before us like a gift. This had to be a private landing, I decided, built by some fisherman from the town.

We dropped to our bellies and slithered through the reeds to the water's edge. The boat swung lazily in an eddy, bumping from time to time against the pilings. Naokan held up five fingers to show me that it would hold us all. I nodded and we scrambled backward to the cover of the trees. Musket and cannon fire shook the air with thunderous bursts. Shouts, the words unintelligible, punctuated the battle, which raged less than a mile away. By now I was driven by only one goal: to get across the river away from this madness, so we could find a safe place to hole up for the night.

When we reached the women, I was relieved to find that my aunt had awakened and was sitting up, cradled in Joanna's arms; but her first words proved that her mind was still muddled.

"Anne, I don't feel well." Her eyes, filled with fear, pleaded with me for help.

I bent over her and touched her hand. "I know. We're going to get you to a place where you can rest."

I gathered up my things, including Naokan's discarded shackles, and once more slung the bag over my shoulder. Together, Joanna and I lifted my aunt to her feet, then half carried, half dragged her toward the river while Naokan and Pomanah hurried ahead to untie the boat.

As we started to lift my aunt into the boat, Joanna glanced downriver and exclaimed, "God have mercy, what's happening?"

The hairs lifted on my arms when I followed her glance to see boats surging out into the current from the Jamestown docks, not just small boats but sloops, as well. For a moment I thought that Berkeley had decided to come upriver and attack Bacon's men on this side of the barricade. Then, as I watched, the boats tacked to the east, heading downriver. I realized then that the musket and cannon fire had lessened, no longer a continuous barrage but irregular bursts of noise. The significance of those fleeing boats suddenly struck me.

"Berkeley's troops—they're abandoning the town!"

"Then you can't cross the river," Joanna said. "If Berkeley catches you over there—"

"If Bacon catches us over here, it will be just as bad."

"Many boats," Naokan said calmly. "They will not see us."

I grasped at once what he meant. "You're right. We'll be lost in the crowd and no one will pay attention to us."

"But when we get across—," Joanna began.

"We won't worry about that yet."

But I did worry about it. Although we tried to angle toward the opposite shore, the current, swollen by runoff from recent rains, dragged us further and further downriver in the wake of Berkeley's troops. Other boats followed behind ours, a regular armada.

We had drifted at least five miles before we finally managed to reach the other shore, where we landed less than three hundred yards from a rowboat that held two of Berkeley's men, poorly dressed as if they might be indentured servants who had followed their masters to join Berkeley's ranks. I knew we presented a strange sight, two white women, a white man and two Susquehannocks, but the men seemed more interested in their own plight than in any threat they may have perceived from us.

Perhaps it was the presence of Aunt Charlotte, obviously an aristocrat in her fine clothes, that allayed their suspicions.

Naokan and I looked at each other. He jerked his head toward the woods, indicating that we should seek cover, and I nodded. He leapt from the boat and secured it to a bush while I helped the women disembark. The voice of one of the men drifted toward us.

"— couldn't believe it when I saw all those white aprons."

"Faugh!" exploded the other. "What a trick, hiding behind women."

"It worked, didn't it?" asked the first man. "Here we are, fleeing like rats, while Bacon takes Jamestown." He laughed and added, "Did you see Berkeley's face when those women appeared in the meadow? I thought he was going to have apoplexy."

While the men lumbered about, slipping in the mud and cursing as they dragged their boat up the bank, we quickly left the shore and headed through the trees. When it became obvious that Aunt Charlotte could no longer walk, even with Joanna's and my help, I handed my bag of tools to Naokan and hoisted Aunt Charlotte into my arms. I'm sure her clothing weighed more than she did, for even through the barrier of silk gown and petticoats I could still tell how slight her body was. My mother had also been slight of build. With a catch in my throat I remembered my last birthday when I had swept up my mother, who had seemed not much bigger than Mary, to swing her round and round the room while my father had clapped his hands and laughed. Her head had dropped onto my shoulder just as Aunt Charlotte's head now nestled into my neck, as trusting as a sleepy child's. I realized that she still did not know who I was.

How far we walked I don't know, but twilight had deepened into dusk by the time Naokan signaled for a halt.

"Lodge," he whispered.

At first I thought he had found the remains of an Indian village, but when I peered through the darkening shadows, I saw that the structure was a log hut. We all stood in silence for several minutes, and I knew that the others were waiting, as I was, for some noise that would betray the presence of another human being. When no sound came to alarm us, we moved closer. Finally Naokan slipped inside and soon emerged to murmur, "Empty."

One by one we entered through the sagging doorway. It took a while for my eyes to adjust, but at last I sensed, rather than saw, that we were in a small room with a fireplace built into one wall. Shadows in the room resolved into a table, a bench, a chest, a narrow cot. Joanna edged forward and sat on the cot, bouncing up and down.

"Yes, it will hold her," she said.

With relief I laid my aunt down on the whispering corn husk mattress. She moaned, rolling her head from side to side.

"Shuuu," I murmured. "You're safe now."

"Safe," she whispered.

"Yes. Try to get some rest."

Again I thought of a trusting child as she nestled into the rough ticking.

"She needs food to build her strength," Joanna said. "I wonder if there's anything to eat in here."

She and Pomanah began searching the room. Naokan stood guard just outside the doorway while I searched, too. The chest yielded a bushel of dried corn only partially nibbled by mice. In the ashes that covered the floor of the fireplace we found a small iron pot.

"Ah," Joanna said, obviously pleased. "Robert, if you'll build a fire and get me some water, we can make corn mush."

I felt my pocket to make certain that I still had my tinderbox, then took the pot and stepped outside to join Naokan. Although he was little more than a shape in the gathering darkness, I saw him lift his head, heard him sniff the wind, which fingered my hair and sighed past my ears like a mournful ghost. I sniffed, too, but smelled nothing.

"Smoke," Naokan said.

He moved to a nearby oak tree and shinnied up the trunk, vanishing into the shadows above. I waited in silence until he slipped back down to join me.

"Big fire," he said, pointing upriver. I put down the pot and climbed to the top of the tree. To the west a false sunset tinged the clouds over the spot where Jamestown should be. The horror that had shaken me when I'd found my home a smoking ruin surrounded by the bodies of my family now shook me again until I almost lost my hold on the tree. I scrambled down to join Naokan.

"The forest burns," he said.

"I think it might be Jamestown." If so, had someone deliberately set the town on fire or had it been an accident? Had Amos escaped?

"We leave soon," Naokan said.

"In the morning," I agreed. "Right now, though, we must feed my aunt. I'll get the water, you get the wood."

Later, with our bellies full of boiled corn, we settled down on the rough floor near the fireplace where a few remaining embers snapped and glowed like bobcats' eyes.

I finally fell into a restless sleep haunted by nightmares filled with flame and flood. Just before dawn I awoke to the sound of rain. A drop of water struck my face, then another and another, dripping through the roof above my head. I sat up to see Joanna peering through the open doorway out into the gray wet dawn.

"We can't take her out in this," she said.

I rose and moved to stand beside her. Together we scanned the lowering sky.

"Looks like the kind of rain that might last for days," I commented.

"That's what I think, too. It's dangerous for you to stay here, dangerous for them." She gestured toward Naokan and

Pomanah, who had awakened and were now sitting up and listening. "The three of you must move on. I'll stay here and take care of her."

"You have no food."

"There is some corn left."

"Not much. You'll need meat. A squirrel or a turkey."

"Then kill a squirrel for me before you go. When the weather clears and she feels better, I'll take her to one of Berkeley's camps."

"What if she dies?"

"Then I'll bury her."

I glanced toward my aunt and saw that her hair had loosened in the night to flow across the mattress in a pale cascade. Sleep had softened the usual harsh lines of her face. She looked vulnerable and young. My heart constricted in my chest: she looked like my mother.

Naokan and Pomanah rose and joined us at the door.

"You go," I said to them. "Go to that cave where we used to meet in the mountains beyond the waterfall. I'll join you there in a few days."

Naokan and Pomanah glanced at each other and then shook their heads.

"We will stay with you," Pomanah told me firmly. To Joanna she added, as she touched the leather pouch that hung around her waist, "Medicine for the fever."

Joanna lifted her chin and straightened her shoulders. "All right, then. We need another fire and a pot of fresh water. Meat, if you can find it."

"We will find it," Naokan promised.

While the women busied themselves near the fireplace, he and I headed out into the rain.

Twenty-one

JUST AS I HAD predicted, the rain settled in to stay. The only comfort I felt lay in the fact that the downpour, which delayed our departure, kept Berkeley's men close to their own camps.

Several days went by during which we fell into a routine that lulled us all, I think, into a false sense of security. Joanna and Pomanah tended my aunt while Naokan and I hunted in the vicinity of the cabin. Although we dared not risk shooting my pistol, which might have alerted others in the forest to our presence, we did manage, at different times, to catch fish. We also snared a partridge, two rabbits, and a squirrel. Joanna cooked these in stews that she flavored with nuts and berries. Meanwhile, Pomanah steeped teas made of wild herbs, which she fed to my aunt throughout each day.

Several times I felt that my aunt was close to death, but she managed each time to rally.

"She has a strong will to live," Joanna said. "Even though she seems to know nothing on the outside, on the inside she is fighting hard. That will save her if anything can."

There came a day, however, when my aunt raved in delirium, calling mostly for my mother but sometimes for her father. Once she even called for Amos.

"I wonder what has happened to Amos," I murmured.

"Maybe he has used all this confusion to escape," Joanna replied. "When the next slave ship comes—"

She broke off and eyed me warily, and I sensed that she felt she had revealed too much.

"He told me his plan," I said. "Don't worry, I won't

betray him. Do you really think he can get away from here and find his own village someday?"

"No. Do you really think you and your two friends can get away from here and find a safe place in the wilderness?"

"We have to try."

"So does he."

My aunt's raving continued throughout that day and night, and I was sure that she would die before dawn. But Joanna and Pomanah tended her faithfully, and by morning her fever had broken. She slept then, a peaceful slumber that lasted for many hours.

By the next day she was able to sit up for a brief while, but she still seemed confused, as if the illness had dazed her senses. She cowered, hands shielding her face, when Pomanah drew near with a cup of medicinal tea.

"No, no, go away," she cried, her voice shaking with fear.

"She doesn't remember you," Joanna said calmly as she took the cup from Pomanah. "Here, I'll give her the tea."

Naokan, who had been out hunting, entered at that moment carrying a dead rabbit by its ears.

"Oh!" cried my aunt, her eyes wide with terror, and I saw that she did not remember him, either.

"It's all right," Joanna said in a soothing voice. "Don't be afraid. Everything is all right."

"But where are we? Why aren't we at home?"

"We took a journey and you got sick. These people took us in and helped us. Now you're getting well. Soon we'll go home again."

As Joanna spoke she threw me a warning glance, which told me, as clearly as words, not to mention that Bacon had taken Jamestown.

Then my aunt's gaze fell on me, and the old pinch-faced anger returned, along with the sour dislike that had been absent from her face during her illness. "Robert! What are you doing here?"

At least she knew me, which I supposed was a good sign.

"How are you feeling, Aunt Charlotte?"

She looked me up and down, her eyes burning with fury, then turned back to Joanna and demanded in an imperious voice, "Take me home at once."

"She's feeling better," Joanna told me with a wry grin.

All resemblance to my mother had vanished from Aunt Charlotte's visage. A sense of loss spread through my chest, bringing with it a dull ache.

"Sunshine. Soon," Naokan said as he placed the rabbit on the hearth.

I glanced toward the doorway and saw that the rain did indeed seem to be slackening.

"Big war chief's camp. That way." He pointed toward the west, then fitted his hands together at an angle that showed me how much distance the sun would have to travel in the sky to get there. Probably a two-hour walk.

"Berkeley?" I asked.

He gave one quick nod of assent.

"I can take over now," Joanna said stoutly. "Robert, you must get away from here. As soon as the sun is out, those soldiers will be scouring the woods for fresh meat."

I knew that she was right. I was not sure, however, that she could get Aunt Charlotte to Berkeley's camp by herself, not when my aunt was still so weak she could barely sit up.

"Look, I'll carry her most of the way," I said. "When I'm sure that you are close enough to reach the camp by yourselves, then I'll leave."

Joanna considered that for a moment in the same matter-of-fact way she considered everything. "Go outside, then, all of you, while I help her wash and get ready."

"What are you talking about? Where are we going?" my aunt demanded.

"We're going to see the governor," Joanna replied.

"Governor Berkeley? Here?" My aunt frowned, obviously perplexed.

"Not here, but nearby."

"And *you.*" Her eyes pierced me like a knife. "You're with that rakehell Bacon. Is he nearby, too?"

"I don't know."

Uneasiness danced down my spine like a skittish mouse. Had Bacon and his men really burned Jamestown? Were they now on this side of the river?

The uneasiness stayed with me as Naokan, Pomanah, and I stepped outside into a thin mist. Overhead a few wispy clouds struggled without success to dominate the sun. Even as we watched, shafts of light broke through and struck the ground around us, turning the mist into a golden curtain that glimmered for a moment and then vanished.

"You must leave now and head for the cave beyond the waterfall," I said. "As soon as I take my aunt to safety, I'll follow you."

Naokan shook his head. "We will not leave you."

"But Bacon could be in these woods, too."

"We will not leave you."

"Then stay here at the cabin and get food ready for the journey. If I'm not back by sundown, you will know something happened to me. Don't wait around after that. Head toward the mountains."

Naokan regarded me with an impassive face. "Would you leave without us, my brother?"

He knew the answer to that, of course.

Nevertheless, I did win the argument to a certain extent. He and Pomanah finally agreed to stay behind since their presence with us in the forest would undoubtedly create more suspicion in some roving soldier's mind than would my presence alone with two white women who were obviously in distress.

Before leaving the cabin, Joanna and I decided upon a story we could tell: she would claim I was her son, and that we were both indentured to my aunt, who had been victimized by Bacon's army. If my aunt refuted that, then we would claim her mind had been affected by the fever.

I asked Joanna for a square of cloth torn from her petticoat. I then mixed ink from charcoal and broth and used a partridge quill to write a deed to my land in her name.

As I handed her the deed, I said, "If Bacon wins, the land is yours. My family is buried at the edge of the clearing. Please tend the graves for me."

Joanna folded the cloth and tucked it inside her bodice. My aunt watched in obvious bewilderment, her brow as furrowed as a new-plowed field.

We set forth to a paean of birdsong. My aunt insisted upon walking by herself, but she had not gone more than ten steps before she collapsed to her knees. I swept her up, despite her protests, and forged ahead over the matted carpet of wet leaves and pine needles while she pummeled me with blows. Fortunately, she was so weak that her fists did little harm. Finally she gave up hitting me, but held herself rigidly in my arms.

"You are a ruffian," she said. "I've known ever since I first set eyes upon you that you would come to no good."

"I am my father's son," I replied.

"And he was a criminal," she announced in triumph, as if that proved her point.

"My mother loved him."

"She was a fool."

"She was happy. Are you happy?"

Her face, already pale, turned as white as bleached linen. "Of course."

"I don't think so. My mother felt sorry for you."

"What are you saying?" She struggled to get down, but I held her fast.

"She told me the story, how the two of you lost your mother when you were young, and how you—only five years older than she was—comforted and cared for her until she grew up. She worshipped you."

Her face crumpled, revealing the vulnerability underneath. "And yet she went away and left me."

"She grieved that you never found the happiness she found. She missed you, and she never stopped loving you."

For a moment her eyes filled with tears. "My Anne," she whispered. Then the vulnerability vanished, replaced by rage so strong that it changed the color of her eyes from blue to purple. "She would have lived had your father not taken her into danger. Put me down."

"All right."

I stood her on the spongy ground while signaling to Joanna not to interfere. My aunt took a few wobbly steps, then paused, weaving on her feet like a drunken person. Her breath came in labored gasps. When she started to fall, I swept her up again and proceeded once more through the forest. She placed her arms against my shoulders and pushed, holding herself as far away from me as she could. She lacked the strength to do that for long and soon she collapsed once more against my shoulder.

We had walked for over an hour when three soldiers appeared suddenly out of the woods, their red, blue, and gold coats gleaming in the sun. They were accompanied by a burly red-bearded man dressed in a black coat and breeches, a man who looked familiar.

"Help me!" my aunt cried as soon as she saw them. "I am being abducted!"

She began to fight again, pounding me with her fists. While I struggled to keep from dropping her, the soldiers drew their guns.

"Put her down," commanded the officer in charge.

Carefully I set her on her feet, but she sank once more to her knees, looking pitiful in her weakness.

Joanna stepped forward, urgently holding out a hand toward the soldiers. "No, don't listen to her. My mistress has had the fever and her mind is wandering. We're bringing her to Berkeley for help. This is my son—"

"That's a lie," said my aunt. "He's not her son, he's with Bacon's army."

"It was Bacon who abducted us, not this boy," cried Joanna desperately. "Bacon dressed us in white aprons, made us stand—"

"You were in the line of white aprons?" asked one of the soldiers.

"Yes," said Joanna. "Oh, Sir, it was a terrible thing. My son managed to rescue us, but then my mistress came down with the fever—"

"Wait a minute, I know you," said the red-bearded man, pointing a finger toward my face. "You *are* with Bacon's army."

"And I know you, too," I said as the memory came back to flood my mouth with the taste of gall. "You held Pomanah while those men tortured Naokan."

Yelling the Susquehannock war cry, I lowered my head and charged.

Twenty-two

PAIN. IT PUSHED against my eyes, my ears, my skull, throbbed with each beat of my heart. I lifted my hands and touched my forehead with tentative fingers, afraid to press too hard.

"Robert."

The sound came from far away, as if the speaker were at the bottom of a well. I didn't answer, unwilling to risk the vibration of my own voice inside my head.

"Robert."

I opened my eyes and blinked against the confusing sight of shadows shot through with dancing stars. A face appeared above me, wavering like smoke.

"Robert, can you hear me?"

I squeezed my eyes shut and swallowed hard against the nausea that threatened to overwhelm me.

"Robert, I don't have much time. Try to wake up."

The voice sounded closer now. I forced my eyes open and watched the face above me solidify from smoke to flesh. Still, the sight did not make sense and I lay there for several seconds before I could accept the truth of the vision.

"Hansford?"

"Yes."

"How—?" I tried to sit up, but the pain drove me back to the floor once more.

"You were clubbed in the head. I was beginning to think you weren't ever going to wake up."

Gingerly I slid my eyes from side to side, still afraid to move my body. "Where? . . ."

"We're locked in a stone barn near the tobacco sheds. He uses it for a gaol."

"Who does?"

"Berkeley."

Moving carefully, I pushed up on my elbows. The hammering inside my head was so loud that I actually seemed to hear it with my ears.

"Berkeley—" I began.

"You fell right into the hornet's nest. This plantation is now his headquarters."

I pushed to a sitting position and leaned forward, resting my head on my knees. "I think my skull is cracked."

"Could be. You've got a knot over your left ear the size of a peach. Robert, why are you still here? I thought you'd be halfway to China by now."

"When my aunt got the fever—"

"You stayed to nurse her." He stated it flatly.

"We found a cabin in the woods. Joanna and Pomanah took care of her while Naokan and I—"

I broke off, remembering that I had told Pomanah and Naokan to leave if I were not back by sundown.

"How long have I been here?" I asked.

"About two hours. They brought you in around noon."

"I have to get out of this place."

I tried to rise, but my arms and legs felt as if they had turned to jelly. Stars again exploded behind my eyes while the room swung back and forth like a pendulum. Hansford gripped my shoulders and held me until the room steadied or else I would have fallen back on the floor. The pounding in my ears sounded even louder. Then I realized the pounding was not coming from inside my skull but from outside the barn.

"Someone is building something," I said.

"Yes," Hansford said.

"I wish they'd stop." A new thought came to me and I wondered why I hadn't asked sooner. "How did you get here?"

"The soldiers caught me yesterday. I was coming through the woods—"

"Alone?"

"Yes. Robert, there's something I have to tell you. That's why I wanted you to wake up before they—"

"Tell me what?" I interrupted, alarmed by his tone.

"Bacon's dead."

My heart jumped, causing the pain to pulse once more inside my head. "How?"

"Fever. I think he was coming down with it even before we took Jamestown. With his death . . . whatever you may have thought of him, Robert, he had an inner power, a fire that kindled those around him. Now that he's gone, everything is in chaos. Many of our men have deserted and gone home."

"Then Berkeley has won."

"Oh, I'm sure the fighting will go on for a while. Our men burned Jamestown to keep Berkeley from returning, and there are still some of our people who want the battle to continue. But it was Bacon the people followed, Bacon who had the vision."

"They'd follow you," I cried. "You're better than Bacon ever was. You saw things he didn't see. He hated all the Indians, but you helped save Pomanah and Naokan—"

"Robert, can you stand up?"

"I don't know. Perhaps if you help me—"

He placed his hands beneath my armpits and lifted while I held on to his arms and forced myself upward. He led me to a small barred window. I blinked against the light and peered toward the sound of hammering. What I saw froze my heart.

I turned to meet Hansford's eyes. "That's a gallows."

He nodded. "It's for me."

Twenty-three

I GRABBED THE EDGE of the window to keep from falling as my knees gave way. A crowd had gathered near the structure: planters dressed in great coats and plumed hats, women wearing silks and laces as if dressed for a party, even children darting about with balls and hoops. A line of soldiers stood at attention to one side while an officer paraded up and down looking them over. The hammering stopped and a cheer went up as a carpenter rose and waved to the crowd to show that he had finished.

"When—"

"They'll be coming for me soon."

I leaned my back against the wall and slid down to sit on the cold stone floor. Hansford sat beside me.

"It's all right, Robert. I've known all along that this could happen."

"But all you were trying to do was make Virginia a better place to live."

"At first, but it got out of hand."

"The things Bacon said, about how Virginia would be better off without England, about how we could do better on our own—"

"I still think that's true. Perhaps we tried for independence too soon. Perhaps one day . . ." He glanced toward me. "Berkeley knows about the oath of allegiance and the names of all those who signed it. He had a spy in our camp."

"A man with a red beard."

"Yes. He was with the soldiers who brought you here."

I absorbed that information while a hollow space expanded behind my heart.

"Then that means . . ."

"He'll hold your trial outside where everyone can hear before he passes sentence. Mine was this morning. I asked to be shot like a soldier, rather than hanged, but he refused."

In my mind I saw Naokan and Pomanah step from the cabin and peer toward the forest, their faces drawn with worry.

Go, I shouted in silence. *Don't wait. Go now!*

Outside the window the officer barked orders to the soldiers.

"Are you afraid?" I asked.

"Not of death itself, but the dying part—he's ordered the short drop."

I knew what that meant. not the swift clean death of the long drop, which broke the neck, but slow death by strangulation as the weight of the body gradually tightened the rope.

"No. Hansford—"

"I'm sorry you didn't get away, Robert. It was a comfort to me to think of you out there headed west."

The officer barked more orders. There came the sound of tramping soldiers, the rat-a-tat of a drum.

"This is it, then," Hansford said calmly.

He rose to his feet and straightened his coat while I worked my way up the wall. Because my head still swam with any sudden movement, I held on to the bars with one hand to keep myself steady.

"You're a good man, Robert," he said.

"I don't think so. Remember when I told you that I no longer know right from wrong?"

"You said other things that day, as well. Perhaps you know more than you think."

The tramping feet arrived outside, then stopped abruptly when a voice shouted, "Company, halt."

Someone fumbled at the door. The bolt slid back and the door swung open. The officer entered, followed by a soldier with a musket tilted over his shoulder.

Ignoring them, Hansford said to me, "Farewell, Robert." Then he smiled. "What is this, the third time we've said goodbye?"

Chin high, back straight, he turned and walked out the door, escorted by the soldier. The officer glanced toward me briefly, his face impassive, before closing and bolting the door.

I turned toward the window, still hanging on while peering toward the crowd. I heard the soldiers maneuver into position outside the door before the officer shouted for them to advance. The drum began a slow muffled cadence, and the soldiers appeared with Hansford walking in the middle, his back still straight, his hands now tied behind him. The crowd parted to let the soldiers through, then closed in again as Hansford climbed the steps to the gallows. He paused beside the hangman and faced the crowd.

I leaned my forehead against the bars and closed my eyes, unable to watch. When another cheer went up, I forced myself to look again. A horseman rode slowly into view and paused before the gallows. It was Berkeley, his stout body dressed in a fine blue coat and breeches, his legs encased in shiny boots with silver buckles. The white plume on his black hat waved gently in the breeze.

"Thomas Hansford, you stand convicted of treason against king and country. Have you anything to say?"

"God is my king. He will be my judge," Hansford answered.

"So be it," said Berkeley.

He motioned to the hangman, who placed a hood over Hansford's head and helped him climb up on a bench. The hangman climbed up beside him and positioned the noose around his neck, then tugged at the rope to make sure it was taut. When the hangman had climbed back down, Berkeley lifted one arm in the air and the drum began to roll. Berkeley dropped his arm, the drum stopped abruptly, and the hang-man jerked the bench from beneath Hansford's feet.

I turned away when he began to struggle.

My trial took place at noon the next day. Berkeley used the scaffold as his platform. When I mounted the steps before all those people to face him, I kept my back straight and my chin high, as Hansford had done, but my knees trembled and my head, still sore, once more began to pound.

Berkeley sat on a tall-backed chair, flanked on either side by Colonel Washington and Philip Ludwell. He eyed me coldly before pronouncing my name.

"Robert Bradford."

"Mr. Berkeley."

I had already decided I would call him neither Governor nor Sir. I braced myself for the words that I knew would come next.

"Mr. Bradford, you stand charged with treason against king and country. How do you plead?"

"Not guilty."

He leaned forward, his brows pulled together in a deep frown. "Did you serve in Bacon's army?"

"Yes."

"Did you spy for Bacon?"

"Yes."

"Did you sign Bacon's oath of allegiance?"

"Yes."

A murmur swept the crowd. I turned and looked them over, recognizing some of the same people who had viewed Hansford's hanging. My breath caught at the sight of Joanna and my aunt standing to one side. Joanna's face signaled sorrow, but my aunt looked as forbidding and tight-lipped as the day Bacon had brought me to her door.

I lifted my eyes above the crowd to gaze toward the

distant rim of blue that marked the mountains to the west. How long had Naokan and Pomanah waited before giving me up? How far had they traveled by now? In my mind I traveled with them past the waterfall, the cliff with the cave, the place where Naokan had been threatened by the bear. What would they find in the mountains beyond? Happiness, I hoped. Peace and safety.

"Mr. Bradford?"

Berkeley's voice penetrated my reverie and brought me back to the reality of this place, this crowd.

"Despite your claim of innocence, you convict yourself by your own admission. Do you have any more to say before I pass sentence?"

Something tugged at my mind, not yet clear but lurking close by if I could only grasp it. I struggled to grab hold, to wrest aside the curtain that kept me from seeing it clearly.

At last, groping for words, I faced Berkeley and said, "My—my father said to do what is right, but deciding what's right isn't always easy. Bacon—he hated all Indians. That was wrong, but he didn't listen and he didn't change. People have tried to tell you how they feel about the king's unfair laws, but *you* don't listen and *you* don't change. I hated all Susquehannocks after they killed my family. Then I found my friends had not taken part, and so I changed. Maybe that's what my father meant. We must do what we think is right, but we must change if we find we are wrong. Berkeley, you're wrong when you don't listen to the people here. Listen to me! Are you listening? I was born in Virginia. *This* is my country, not England. What happens here should be up to me." I gestured toward the crowd. "And to them, not to some king who doesn't give a damn. Bacon said it, and about that he was right!"

No one moved, no one spoke. Into that silence spilled the song of a meadowlark.

Berkeley stirred, as if released from a spell. "Robert Bradford, I sentence you to hang in the morning at dawn, and may God have mercy on your soul."

A soldier mounted the steps and took my arm. For a moment I met Washington's eyes. He held my gaze, his face neither friendly nor accusing but thoughtful, and I felt he might have spoken to me had we been in a different place. The moment passed when the soldier pulled me away and down the steps.

The members of the crowd, still silent, drew back as the soldier, now accompanied by other guards, led me toward the barn. I passed so close to my aunt that I could have reached out and touched her, but no movement of her hands, no flicker of compassion in her eyes, encouraged me to take such a liberty. Joanna also stood without giving any outward sign that she knew me, although grief clouded her face. I thought perhaps she was afraid to acknowledge me now, afraid to run the risk of being branded a traitor, too. Not wanting to compromise her safety, I said nothing, but moved on.

Once inside the barn, the guards led me again to the small room that served as the gaol. They shoved me inside, slammed the door, and shot the bolt into place.

As their footsteps retreated, one of them called, "See you in Hell."

Twenty-four

NOW THE NIGHT is nearly over. I used up all the paper long ago and the candle guttered out shortly thereafter. Sitting here in the darkness while reviewing these memories, I have reached at last a feeling of peace. When my father told me to do what is right, he did indeed mean for me to follow my conscience as I saw it, even if it meant I had to stand alone.

At dawn I will stand in the loneliest place of all. But I won't be alone for my father and Hansford will stand with me.

The owl no longer calls. Perhaps it was frightened away by the woman who arrived earlier to keep the guard company out in the hallway. Their low laughter, the murmur of their voices, has seeped under the door from time to time, although I could not make out their words. Their laughter stopped a while ago and since then they have been silent.

But no, the bolt slides back. Is it time? The night is still dark. Why have the soldiers come so soon? I grab up the papers and stuff them inside my shirt.

The door creaks open and someone enters. A shape, barely discernable in the gloom. A woman. As she comes closer, I can just make out the long tousled hair, the ghostly white of the bodice, which droops from her shoulders in wanton disarray.

"Robert," she whispers.

I draw back in surprise. Who is she? Then I know.

"Joanna."

"Come quickly."

"What—"

"Don't ask questions. Come."

She turns and hurries from the cell. Caught by her

urgency, I follow. No candle burns in the hallway and I almost trip over the body that sprawls on the floor.

Startled, I ask, "Is he—?"

"He's asleep, but we don't know how long the potion will last. Hurry."

We?

Two more shapes step from the shadows.

"Brother," says Naokan.

"She brewed herbs to make a sleeping draught," Joanna whispers, pointing toward Pomanah. "We mixed it with the wine I brought to the guard."

"Come," says Naokan.

He and Pomanah slip through the doorway, and Joanna and I follow. We hurry past the tobacco sheds to a copse beyond. As we enter the shadows another figure appears and holds out a bag.

"Food," she says. "A pistol, hunting knives."

Surprise stiffens my spine. "Aunt Charlotte!"

"What you did for me when I was ill . . . I'm beginning to remember." She thrusts the bag into my hand. "Go quickly before someone comes."

"Are you coming with us?" I ask Joanna.

"No."

"But you'll get in trouble for helping me."

"The guard won't recognize me tomorrow."

"If he does," says Aunt Charlotte, "I will claim that Joanna was caring for me all night. Fever. It sometimes comes back. Berkeley will not dare dispute my word."

"Thank you," I say. The words seem inadequate.

She reaches out and touches my arm, one quick brush of the fingertips that I barely feel through my sleeve.

"I could not let Anne's son hang. Now go."

"Godspeed, Robert," whispers Joanna, and she leans to kiss my cheek.

My aunt snorts with impatience. "Joanna, we must get home. The soldiers will be up soon."

They move away and vanish, swallowed by the night.

"We must go, too," says Naokan.

Our moccasins whisper as we hurry through the woods. Inside my shirt the papers also whisper. I pull them forth and stuff them deep into the bag where they won't fall out and get lost. When we reach the safety of the mountains, I will use these pages to teach my friends to read and write. One day we will finish this story together as we try to make sense of these terrible, bloody months.

Naokan, my enemy, my brother. This is for you.

Author's Note

I first learned of Bacon's Rebellion many years ago while reading to my children from *The Golden Book History of the United States*. There were three pages about the rebellion, along with an illustration of Bacon and his men setting Jamestown on fire. The next day I drove to a nearby university and read everything about the subject I could find.

This interest in history goes back to my own parents, who taught me early on to see the drama that lies behind historical facts.

"History is not just about battles and dates and old men in weird costumes doing noble things," they told me. "History is about real people, including children, caught up in situations that disrupted their lives, often because of some leader's greed or envy or hatred or lust."

So I learned to read between the lines of my history textbooks, and I decided that my parents were right.

After I started researching Bacon's Rebellion, my husband and I took our children to visit Jamestown. There I explored the excavations of the early town and walked among the graves of some of the people who had figured in the rebellion. Afterward I wrote a stage play about the rebellion, as well as a made-for-television movie. These dramas were never produced.

A part of the problem with the plays lay in the fact that both Bacon and Berkeley were seriously flawed. I could not, in good conscience, make either one of them a hero. That's when my parents' words came back to me and I decided to write a story about an ordinary boy who gets caught in the middle between these two fanatical men.

Once I'd made that decision, I then asked myself the following question: "What are the worst things that could happen to this boy?"

And the answer came: "His family gets massacred. He joins Bacon's army. He is captured by Berkeley and sentenced to hang."

Writing a novel set in the past is different from writing historical nonfiction. Nonfiction deals strictly with facts. In fiction the author concentrates on one main character and the way in which personal problems combined with outside events affect that character's actions and emotions. Although it is important for the author to know as much as possible about the history of the period, some of the events must be left out and others expanded or condensed in time in order to structure the book. The novel gives the essence of the story, not the total picture.

Nevertheless, before starting to write this novel I studied in depth a number of historical accounts. (See Bibliography.) Of particular interest were the insights provided by modern historian Stephen Saunders Webb in his book, *1676–The End of American Independence*. Webb draws numerous parallels between the Bacon Rebellion and the American Revolution and concludes that the events of 1676 forecast those of 1776. Also of great help was *Old Virginia and Her Neighbors*, by John Fiske, which not only gives a graphic account of the rebellion, but presents in detail the political and social climate of Virginia throughout the seventeenth century. *The History and Present State of Virginia*, by Robert Beverley, first published in 1705, provides a near-contemporaneous account of the Indians of Virginia during the seventeeth century, while *The Narratives of the Insurrections, 1675–1690*, edited by Charles Andrews, contains eyewitness accounts of the rebellion written by people who were personally involved.

Because an author must pick and choose only those events

that are important to the novel, interesting points sometimes get omitted, such as the following curious facts:

1. During 1675, three portentous events occurred in Virginia, disturbing colonists as well as Indians. One was a large comet, which appeared every evening for a week in the western sky. Another was swarms of "flies," each insect about an inch long, which rose out of spigot holes in the earth and ate the leaves from the tops of the trees. The third was a flight of pigeons, filling a quarter of the sky and flowing from horizon to horizon for several hours. Awed by such sights, colonists recalled that a similar flight of pigeons had appeared in Virginia in 1640 just before a massacre by the Indians. They correctly predicted that the Indian attacks would be renewed.

2. Although Berkeley was himself an educated man who wrote plays that were produced at Greenspring, he did not approve of public education or freedom of the press. He is quoted as saying of Virginia, "I thank God there are no free schools nor printing." He was no doubt influenced by King Charles II, who limited the licensing of newspapers in England because he felt they might dispense seditious information. There was no newspaper printed in Virginia until the 1740s. By 1776, however, the colonists considered freedom of the press and freedom of speech so important that they included both in Article I of the Bill of Rights.

3. Berkeley, a staunch royalist who equated Bacon with Oliver Cromwell, exacted harsh punishment on all the rebel leaders whom he caught after Bacon's death. Most of the rebels were hanged within hours after capture, often without a trial. When William Drummond was captured, Berkeley personally stripped a ring from Drummond's finger, a ring that had been a gift from Drummond's wife, and placed the ring on his own hand. He then ordered Drummond to be drawn and quartered. One hundred years later, the men who drafted the Bill of Rights, remembering such atrocities, included in Article VIII the provision that no one should be subjected to "cruel and unusual punishment."

(During the Jamestown excavations of 1954–56, the bones of a man's leg and foot, along with one-half of his pelvis, were found at the bottom of an old well. Some have speculated that this could be part of Drummond's body.)

4. When the king's troops arrived in Virginia following the end of the rebellion, the colonists were forced to house and feed the soldiers at their own expense. Even those Virginians who had remained loyal to England during the rebellion were angered by this imposition. The memory of this injustice was still fresh enough in the minds of Virginians one hundred years later for them to add Article III to the Bill of Rights, which says that no soldier shall, in time of peace, be quartered in any house without the consent of the owner.

5. After the defeat of the rebels, Berkeley returned
to England where he expected to be honored by
King Charles II. Instead, the king denounced
Berkeley, calling him an old fool for having
"hanged more men in that naked country" than
the king himself had hanged for the murder of his
father. Berkeley died in July 1677, a broken man.
Lady Berkeley later married Philip Ludwell

Glossary

baldric—A belt, usually of ornamented leather, worn diagonally across the chest to support a sword, drum, or bugle.

breastwork—A temporary, quickly constructed fortification, usually breast high.

breechclout—A cloth worn to cover the loins.

breeches—Trousers extending to or just below the knee.

Cavalier—A supporter of Charles I of England, in his struggles against Parliament, and Oliver Cromwell, during the civil war in England, seventeenth century.

cockade—A rosette or knot of ribbon worn especially on the hat as a badge.

draw and quarter—To hang, cut down while still alive, disembowel, and dismember.

firedog—An andiron.

fletch—To feather an arrow.

gaol—Variant spelling of *jail*. (Chiefly British)

homespun—A plain, coarse woolen cloth made of homespun yarn.

indenture—A contract binding one party into the service of another for a specified term.

leggings—Leg coverings of material such as canvas or leather.

moccasin—A soft leather slipper worn by early Native Americans.

musket— A smoothbore shoulder gun used from the late sixteenth through the eighteenth centuries.

popinjay—A vain, supercilious person; a fop.

quill—A writing pen made by sharpening the shaft of a feather.

quiver—A portable case for arrows.

rampart—A fortification consisting of an elevation or embankment.

redemptioner—In Colonial America, an emigrant from Europe who paid for his/her voyage by serving as a bond servant for a specified period.

sloop—A single-masted, fore-and-aft-rigged sailing boat.

Susquehannock —"People of the Falls" or "roily water people." Native Americans, eastern seaboard. (Also spelled Susquehannough, Susquehannah, Susquehanna.)

tinder—Readily combustible material, such as dry grass or twigs.

tinderbox—A small metal box containing flint, steel, and tinder for starting fires.

zounds—Also *swounds*. Used to express anger, surprise, or indignation. (Euphemism for "God's wounds")

Bibliography

Andrews, Charles McLean, ed. *Narratives of the Insurrections, 1675–1690.* (New York: Charles Scribner's Sons, 1915; copyright renewed by Barnes and Noble, Inc., 1943; reprinted 1959).

Beverley, Robert. *The History and Present State of Virginia.* Edited by Louis B. Wright. (Chapel Hill: University of North Carolina Press, 1947).

Bridenbaugh, Carl. *Jamestown 1544–1699.* (Oxford: Oxford University Press, 1980).

Cotter, John L., and J. Paul Hudson, *New Discoveries at Jamestown.* (Washington, DC: U.S. Government Printing Office, 1957).

Craven, Wesley Frank. *The Southern Colonies in the Seventeenth Century, 1607–1689.* (Baton Rouge: Louisiana State University Press and the Littlefield Fund for Southern History of the University of Texas, 1970).

Davis, J. E. *Jamestown and Her Neighbors.* (Richmond: Garrett and Massie Pub., 1928).

Fiske, John. *Old Virginia and Her Neighbors.* 2 vols. (Boston: Houghton Mifflin and Company, 1897).

Hatch, Charles E. *Jamestown, Virginia, the Townsite and Its Story.* The U.S. Government Printing Office: The National Park Service Historical Handbook Series No. 2, (Washington, DC, 1949).

McCary, Ben C. *Indians in Seventeenth-Century Virginia.* (Charlottesville: The University Press of Virginia, 1957).

Middlekauff, Robert. *Bacon's Rebellion.* Charles Sellers, ed. (Chicago: Rand McNally & Company, 1964).

Sparks, Jared, ed. *The Biography of Nathaniel Bacon, 1648–1676,* by William Ware, 1797–1856, The Library of American Biography, 2nd series, vol. 3. (Boston: Little, Brown and Company, 1864).

Tyler, Annie Tucker. *"Thomas Hansford, the First Native Martyr to American Liberty"* (pp 193–201). *Richmond, VA: Virginia Historical Society Collections*, vol. xi.

Washburn, Wilcomb E. *The Governor and the Rebel, A History of Bacon's Rebellion in Virginia.* (Chapel Hill: University of North Carolina Press, 1957).

Webb, Stephen Saunders. *1676, the End of American Independence.* (New York: Alfred A. Knopf, 1984).

Wertenbaker, Thomas Jefferson. *Torchbearer of the Revolution: The Story of Bacon's Rebellion and Its Leader.* (New Jersey: Princeton Univerity Press, 1940).